A
Captivating
Touch

Elsa Winckler

A Captivating Touch
Copyright © 2021 Elsa Winckler
All rights reserved.

ISBN: (ebook) 978-1-953335-20-3
(print) 978-1-953335-36-4

Inkspell Publishing
207 Moonglow Circle #101
Murrells Inlet, SC 29576

Edited By Rie Langdon
Cover Art By Najla Qamber

To Theo who captivated my heart all those years ago

ELSA WINCKLER

CHAPTER 1

"I'm sorry, but I don't trust a man who shaves his legs," Caitlin said, cradling the cell phone against her shoulder while flexing her fingers. She'd been massaging cyclists for the better part of thirty minutes.

It was the end of the second day of the grueling annual Wines to Whales cycling race, which had started at Lourensford Estate in Somerset West, situated less than an hour's drive from Cape Town. She and the other two physiotherapists on duty had not been all that busy the previous day. Only a few cyclists with minor injuries had come to see them but from their experience the previous year, they had known the second day would take its toll on the cyclists.

The physio team had been treating a steady stream of riders with back pain, knee injuries, and hip problems. When Dana phoned, Caitlin had just finished with a patient and for the moment, at least, it was quiet. The other two therapists were busy on the far side of the big tent.

"You, my friend, don't trust men, period. There is a very good reason cyclists shave their legs; as a physiotherapist who often works on them, you should

1

know that." Dana giggled over the phone.

"Yes, I know shaved legs are easier to treat when there are wounds, but really? A man should have hair on his legs. It's just a given."

"You get to put your hands on gorgeous, virile, sexy cyclists in tight shorts and you want to complain?" Dana sounded exasperated.

"Sexy? Cyclists? Seriously? They all look the same. Underfed, sinewy, and hairless. There is nothing sexy about a man who looks like that. And virile? I don't know about that. Sitting on a saddle all day—"

Caitlin heard a movement behind her. "Got to go," she quickly said to Dana and turned around. And blinked. A big, sweaty, sexy, gorgeous-looking cyclist with ink-black hair and chocolate brown eyes was standing just inside the tent, his helmet tucked under his arm. If the frown between his eyes was anything to go by, he was seriously ticked off.

Without consciously thinking about it, she dropped her gaze down to his legs. They were dirty and okay, hairless, but all muscle. Sexy, rippling muscle. He moved slowly toward her, the tight shorts leaving very little to her overactive imagination.

"I'm looking for a physio," he said brusquely.

She looked up. "I'm a physio. Can I help you?" she asked, trying to sound professional.

"If you're quite sure you've finished with your fascinating phone conversation," he said.

Swallowing a quick retort, she tried to hold back her rising annoyance. He might be gorgeous to look at, but what a rude man. She ignored the sarcastic comment and motioned him to one of the high beds on which they worked.

"Back?" she asked.

"Yeah," he said and nodded, looking even more irritated.

"Please take off your shirt and lie down on your

stomach," Caitlin said and turned away, looking for the massage oil.

"Any pain in your legs?" she asked as she turned back to him. And nearly dropped the bottle of oil she was holding.

On the same level as her eyes was the most perfect six-pack of steel muscles she had ever seen. And if she hadn't been holding something in her hand, she would probably have done something stupid like putting out a hand and touching him to make sure his abs really felt as hard as they looked.

"The pain kind of goes down into my right buttock," he said, bringing her back to reality.

What was she thinking? She stepped back quickly and turned her back on him again.

"Okay, please lie down," she mumbled while frantically looking for something else to do. A towel. She would need a towel. There was a sound behind her, and praying that the man was lying down, she once more turned around, this time slowly.

He was stretched out on his stomach. His broad, muscled back was as impressive as the six-pack in front. Her hands tingled as if she were already touching him. *Oh, my goodness. It is so hot in here all of a sudden.*

Caitlin exhaled slowly. She was a trained professional. Treating injuries was what she'd studied so hard for and what she wanted to do. *He is just another patient. In pain.* She was supposed to help him, not drool over him.

"You have probably overstretched the ligaments, causing them to overstrain," she said, trying to focus on what she was doing, not what she wanted to be doing.

His head turned. "You think?" Sarcasm dripped from his words.

"Yes, I think," she snapped. "You guys should all learn to change your riding position."

"Will you just give me a massage? Please? Lower back." He turned his head again.

Caitlin gnashed her teeth in an effort to keep quiet. Any wayward thoughts she had about the man vanished. Could one person be so obnoxious and irritating? She normally made light conversation with her patients, but if he didn't want that, fine. She poured some of the oil onto her palm.

As she brought her hands down onto his lower back, she steeled herself. Any second now she was going to touch him. Annoyed, she shook her head. She was a trained physiotherapist for goodness' sake, not a masseuse in a sleazy joint. And then her hands were on his back, kneading and massaging muscles hard as steel.

***

Don swallowed a groan. Heavenly. She talked too much, but what she did with her hands was absolutely heavenly. He had to have pulled a muscle when he'd lifted his bike from his brother's pickup that morning. At the time, he hadn't taken much notice. He'd been too excited to start the second leg of the race.

In order to get some much-needed exercise, he'd taken up cycling again two years before. At that point, his three brothers had joined his boutique hotel group after doing their own thing for a while, and for the first time in ten years he had time again to exercise regularly. Together they now owned several hotels scattered throughout South Africa and the Seychelles. Because his brothers were now co-owners, he could actually take time off from work without having to worry about anything. One of his brothers would be there to handle any crisis.

They all loved cycling, had done it since school, and now belonged to the same cycling club. Out on the dirt roads, they were not the Cavallo tycoons; they could just be ordinary people, a luxury they all coveted.

He'd done this particular race the previous year and when he told his brothers about it, they were all eager to join him. They all planned to take part in the Cape Epic race in March next year and this race was part of their training.

He had promised them the thrill of a lifetime. The challenge today, as he had explained to Darryn, Dale, and David, was conquering three linked, manmade tracks. The 65-kilometer loop included 1200 meters of climbing without a flat section in sight.

The start before they hit the open roads had been fast and tricky, but once they had gained the altitude for the day, it was playtime. They had dropped over the top stile at Oak Valley and had nailed the descent in the area, a swooping one that had culminated in a mad sprint along the river while dodging trees and cows.

And it was only when the adrenaline had settled down that he'd realized his back was acting up. By that time he'd left his brothers far behind. Now if this cutie pie would just hurry up and stop talking, he could be feeling better before his brothers found out that he had a problem. Otherwise, he'd never hear the end of it.

The hands that were massaging his painful muscles were soft but very focused on what they were doing. She had been standing behind him but was now moving to his side. She bent forward to add more pressure and the subtle smell of violets and roses surrounded him.

Every rational thought fled from his mind. Those soft hands on his lower back were relaxing his muscles but wreaking havoc on the rest of his body. Every touch left him craving more and his anxious thought was that she should never stop what she was doing.

She lifted her hands and he opened his eyes and looked at her. She hooked her thumbs into the elastic of his shorts and pulled it down a few centimeters. Her hands trembled slightly before she pressed firmly on his sore muscles. This time his groan escaped.

Her gaze flew to his. "I'm sorry," she said and lifted her hands quickly.

"Don't stop," he managed through clenched teeth.

She put more oil on her hands and started again on his lower back. He closed his eyes again. Slowly, very slowly, her hands moved over his lower back until she was once more massaging his right buttock. Firm fingers worked his sore muscles, lifted and pressed down again. And each time they moved ever so slightly toward his front.

If he'd moved only slightly, she could... Oh, bloody hell, what was he thinking? He had to get up from the bed in a few minutes. At the rate his body was reacting to this woman, he wouldn't be able to stand, let alone walk out of there.

There was a commotion outside the tent and then he heard his brothers' voices. Damn.

"There he is," Dale called out.

"Doesn't look to me as if he's in pain," Darryn said.

"Nope, I agree," David added.

Don lifted his head and glared at his brothers. The girl pulled his shorts up and turned to them.

"Can I help you?" she asked in a clipped voice.

"No, gorgeous, we're fine. But then, we're younger than our big brother here. Thank you for helping him. Does he have to go to the hospital?" David asked innocently.

Don swung his legs from the bed and grabbed his shirt. "Very funny," he snarled. But it was a good thing his brothers had interrupted the massage. Their presence achieved what only a pail of cold water would have been able to do otherwise. At least now he'd be able to stand up.

He turned to the physiotherapist. "Thank you—"

"I'm not done—" she said.

"I'm fine," he interrupted and turned to leave.

"You can't leave, Don, you haven't introduced us to this beautiful girl," Darryn complained, putting a hand to his back. "Now that I think about it, I also have a pain right here," he said with a big smile.

"And you know, my leg is acting up—" began Dale.

"Will you guys drop it?" Don snarled. "She doesn't even like cyclists. Isn't that right Miss…?"

Her eyes narrowed momentarily, but then she turned to his brothers with a big smile. "I'm Caitlin Sutherland. And I never said I don't like cyclists."

David stuck out his hand. "I'm David Cavallo. This is Darryn, that one is Dale, and grumpy here is Don, our oldest brother. It's good to meet you. Are you from around here?"

Don wanted to strangle David. And his two other brothers. They had formed a circle around the girl and were all but salivating over her.

"Sorry to disappoint you, but Ms. Sutherland doesn't trust men who shave their legs," he interrupted. "She sees us as underfed, sinewy, and hairless—isn't that how you put it, Ms. Sutherland?" Before she could say anything, he turned to his brothers. "Come on, we have to go."

"I'm from Hermanus," the girl said, ignoring him completely. "I've just opened my own physiotherapy rooms there. This is the second year I've been asked to help during this race."

"Hermanus?" echoed Darryn. "Don here has inherited a house in Hermanus, so we're there often."

"House is a kind word for that pile of bricks," Dale said. "But we're helping him to fix up the place." He stepped closer to her. "Do you have a business card with your details? You never know, we might just need a physiotherapist soon," he said.

She handed one over, smiling sweetly for his brothers. Don swallowed his irritation.

"So, we'll see you around, Caitlin Sutherland." David smiled. "Come on guys, let's get this old man to bed," he joked and slapped Don on the back.

"Go ahead, I'll be with you shortly." Don turned back to the girl. Caitlin. The name suited her. His brother was right. She was gorgeous.

"Thank you," he said.

"I haven't finished," she repeated.

"I'm fine. My back is feeling better already."

"You should have at least two more sessions with a physio. Make an appointment with your own as soon as possible."

He nodded but didn't walk away. She bit her lip. So, Miss Cool was nervous around him. The thought made him smile for the first time since he'd walked into the tent. He moved a little closer to her. Violet blue. Her eyes were violet blue.

Her honey-brown hair was tied back but a tendril had escaped. He tucked the lock behind her ear. Then he bent down.

"And just so you know," he said softly, "there is nothing wrong with my virility."

Her eyes widened and she opened her mouth to say something, but he quickly turned away. Just before he ducked out of the tent, he looked back. She was staring after him.

***

Caitlin slumped against the bed. She felt lightheaded. The whole tent was still sizzling with testosterone. The Cavallo brothers packed a hell of a punch. Like Don, his brothers also had black hair and brown eyes. Probably an Italian mother or father, would be her guess. And heavens, were they built.

She stood up and began tidying the bed. They were all gorgeous, but it was Don who occupied her mind. She remembered every stroke of her hand on his lower back, remembered how his skin felt under her fingers, remembered the heat in his eyes when he had turned to look at her...

Voices from the entrance of the tent brought her back to earth. Two more cyclists came in. She was there to work.

CHAPTER 2

"Are you sure I can go?" Maggie asked, sniffling.

Caitlin gently pushed her receptionist toward the door. "Maggie, you're ill. Go to bed. I'm sure I'll be able to cope without a receptionist for one Friday afternoon." Caitlin smiled. "Besides, there are no further appointments, so I'm going to write on my blog—"

Maggie turned around quickly. "You have one appointment. Someone phoned…I'm sorry, I didn't write it down."

"It's fine, I can handle one patient. What time?" she asked and walked to her appointment book.

"Only at five. I'm so sorry—"

"Go, Maggie. It just means I have more time to write. I don't mind staying later."

When Maggie finally left, Caitlin took the elastic off her ponytail and walked to the window. She combed her fingers through her hair.

She'd opened her rooms in September and had been just in time to watch the annual arrival of the whales in these waters. From her second-story window she had a wonderful view over the whole of Walker Bay.

With a smile she walked back to her laptop. She had

the office to herself and couldn't wait to blog. She hadn't had a chance to update it since the previous weekend, and wanted to catch up with her readers.

At first, the blog had been her way of venting about her latest disastrous date. Fed up with the way she'd been treated, she'd started to write about the types of men girls out there on the dating circuit should steer clear of. To her amazement and delight, it seemed as if her writing had triggered something in many women and the blog had somehow gotten a life of its own.

She wrote about all kinds of men, but she had something of a mental block when it came to soulmates, to the notion that some man out there was "the one." Probably because she didn't believe they existed. In her experience "the one" was an ideal, invented by romance writers like her mother, and rom-com movies.

Chocolate brown eyes. She grimaced. It had been nearly a week and she still remembered the cyclist she'd treated the previous Saturday. Don. At the oddest times she would think about him, would worry about his back, would wonder whether he'd seen another physiotherapist.

She didn't know the man from Adam, but she'd been having X-rated dreams about him all week. In her line of work, she treated attractive men every day. Why she couldn't get this particular one out of her head was a mystery.

Her cell phone rang. Smiling, she picked it up. "Hi, Mum. You've been very quiet. Busy with another book?"

"I have just sent it off to the publishers and—"

"Now you're phoning your daughters to find out what is going on in their love lives?" Caitlin asked, laughing.

"Well, I've written stories about the love lives of all my friends and their children. I can't believe none of my three beautiful daughters is able to find a man."

"Oh, we're able. Just not willing."

Her mother sighed loudly on the other end of the phone. "Not all men are like your father, my dear girl.

Please remember that. There are good men out there. Plenty of them. Men are human and like us, they make mistakes. You have to forgive your father at some point, sweetheart. Talk to him."

Caitlin shook her head. "You're a better person than me, Mum. I talk to him. He phones me on my birthday. But I just don't have anything to say to him. How are Zoe and Hannah? I miss my sisters—"

"Oh, yes, Zoe told me you helped with the Wines to Whales race. All those sweaty, strong cyclists…surely there must have been one who needed your help? In tight shorts? Didn't anyone heat your blood?"

"Mum!" Caitlin gasped.

"What? I'm old, my dear, not dead. Now, tell me."

Caitlin heard footsteps outside her rooms. "I have a client, Mum. I'll talk to you later. And just so you know, I'd never fall for a cyclist. They shave their legs," she joked before she put the phone down.

When she turned, the door to her rooms opened and Don Cavallo stood there. The atmosphere in the room changed instantly. For a full minute, all she could do was stare while her brain frantically tried to process what she should do next. And even before she could make sense of what was going on, her hormones sprang to attention. Her heart raced, her blood surged through her body, her hands felt clammy.

When he'd been wearing his tight cycling shorts, he had been very sexy, but cleaned up and dressed in a black T-shirt and jeans, he packed a sexual punch that left her short of breath and wanting…something. Did she know him from somewhere else? He looked vaguely familiar.

He closed the door behind him. "What is your problem with shaved legs?" he asked, clearly annoyed.

Caitlin blinked and stood up quickly. "Why do you listen to other people's conversations?" She folded her arms. Irritated with her reaction to this man, she tried to compose herself.

He kept frowning at her.

"Can I help you?" she asked in her most professional voice.

He cocked an eyebrow. "I've made an appointment to see you this afternoon." He looked at his watch. "But I am early and you're clearly very busy. I'll find someone else," he said, turning turned to leave.

Caitlin was speechless. Had Maggie mentioned who her appointment was? She struggled to remember their conversation but at this point everything was a blank. The door was closing.

"Wait!" she called out. Don turned. "Look, I'm sorry. I sent the receptionist home. She has a dreadful cold. Please come in."

Don put his hands in his pockets. "This was not a good idea—"

"You made an appointment. You're here, I'm here. You can go through that door," she interrupted, pointing toward one of the treatment rooms. She tried her best professional voice. "Take off your shirt and lie down. I'll be with you shortly."

Only when she heard the door close behind him did she exhale slowly. She always told her patients which pieces of clothing to take off, so why did it sound sexual when she told Don to take off his shirt? She couldn't think when the man was around. He literally took her breath away.

And no, she hadn't imagined the instant attraction she'd felt when she'd treated him before. There was nothing imaginary about her reaction. Just the thought that she would be touching him in a few minutes had her mouth watering. How on earth was she going to survive the ordeal?

***

Why the hell had he made this appointment? Don

tossed his T-shirt on the chair and lay down on the bed.

When he'd seen her on Saturday, her hair had been tied back and she'd been dressed casually. But today, her light brown tresses were loose, falling messily over one shoulder. A frilly kind of top hugged her curves in all the right places.

He'd steeled himself not to react to the picture he'd had of her in his head. And then he opened the door and there she was, all mussed up and looking sexy. For one insane moment, he'd wanted to draw her close, devour her mouth, and push his fingers through her hair.

This had been such a bad idea. He should have gone to his own physiotherapist during the week. She was gray, a granny, and knew exactly what to do. But then he'd found Caitlin's business card in his wallet. One of his brothers had probably put it there.

Don grimaced. He had an explanation of why he was in Hermanus, although deep down he knew he was looking for an excuse to see this woman again. It had been a crazy week with complications at all their hotels so it was easy to persuade himself that it would make more sense to wait until the weekend. He knew about a physiotherapist in Hermanus, he'd argued.

But he should not have come. Not after the way the previous session had haunted his dreams. He'd struggled to sleep during the week and when he'd finally managed to drift off, the imagined whisper of her hands had been all over his body. Caressing him, stroking him.

He shifted uncomfortably. He was turned on already and she hadn't touched him yet. How the hell was he supposed to survive this?

The door opened. He turned his head to look at her. She'd tied her hair back again. Good. He closed his eyes.

***

"How…" Caitlin cleared her throat. Damn it, she

couldn't even talk near the man. "How is the pain?" She tried again as she poured oil on her hand.

He just grunted and for another second, she hovered her hands over his body. And then she was touching him, massaging and molding his flesh. She tried to focus on what she was supposed to be doing. Easing his pain, helping his body to heal.

But her hands seemed to have forgotten that they should listen to her brain. They were doing all kinds of things her brain definitely hadn't told them to do.

For one, they started on his shoulders, which wasn't anywhere near his lower back. They took their time working on the hard muscles across the trapezius. Then, reluctantly, she moved down, centimeter by centimeter, exploring each and every contour of his body along the way.

When she came to his middle, her fingers somehow just slipped down and found their way around his body so that she could also touch part of the obliques in the front of his body. For long minutes, her hands stayed there, massaging, stroking, until she could feel a quiver just below his skin.

It was as if she was floating high above him and was watching someone else working on him. She moved her hands to his back, shifted them farther down over warm skin while kneading and caressing every part they came into contact with.

When she reached the top of his jeans, her fingers simply slipped underneath the belt. And for endless minutes, they went on to explore the flesh and muscles they found there. His skin was becoming warmer and warmer to her touch. In fact, he was burning up.

Her hands stilled and she pulled them out of his pants, her face flaming.

"I…" She swallowed. Her throat was so dry. "I think that should do it," she finally managed.

It was only then she heard voices coming from the

direction of the reception area.

Grateful for the interruption, she moved toward the door.

"You can get dressed. I'll see you outside," she said over her shoulder.

"I'll be there in a minute," he said through clenched teeth.

She glanced back worriedly. He sounded as if he was in pain.

"Are you okay? Is something wrong? Did I hurt you?" she asked anxiously.

He lifted his head and with just one steamy look, she knew why he wasn't getting up. She felt the heat spread to her face.

"Exactly," he said.

She fled.

What had possessed her to touch him like that? She was a professional, damn it. In all the time she'd been a physiotherapist, this had never happened to her. She'd never even come close to doing such a thing. He had to be wondering whether she gave massages like that to everyone.

"Hi! Why are you so flustered?" asked Zoe. She and Hannah were standing in the reception area.

Caitlin came to an abrupt halt and nearly groaned out loud. Her two sisters were staring at her. Her heart was still racing and her hormones, which had gone completely haywire while she was massaging Don, still hadn't settled down.

"What are you doing here?" she finally managed, hugging her sisters and trying not to sound as rattled as she was feeling.

"I'm back from France and will be staying with Mum for a few days. I've picked up Zoe, we've phoned Dana, and we were hoping you could join us for coffee," Hannah said. She put a hand to Caitlin's forehead. "But you look feverish. Are you okay? Have you seen a doctor—?"

The door opened behind them and Caitlin wished she could disappear into thin air. She was never going to hear the end of this.

"Oh my," Zoe breathed, "and who have you been hiding in that room?"

Caitlin gulped in some air. "This…this is Don Cavallo, a client. I…treated him last weekend during the Wines to Whales race. He was one of the cyclists. Don, these are my sisters, Zoe and Hannah."

"Oh," said Zoe with a big smile, and held out her hand. "So pleased to meet you, Don."

Hannah stared at him and frowned. "Cavallo? Any relation to Darryn Cavallo?"

"Yes, he's my brother," Don said. "Do you know him?"

Hannah's lips thinned. "He used to be a photographer. I'm a model. We've met," Hannah said, her voice cool. "We'll be at the Burgundy," she said to Caitlin. "We've phoned Dana already. Join us when you can." And before Caitlin could reply, she'd grabbed Zoe by the arm and the door closed behind them.

"What was that about?" Don asked, voicing her own thoughts.

"I have no idea. Hannah is the quiet sister and hardly ever gets angry. Your brother must have done something she didn't like."

"Or she could be the one who did something," Don said.

Irritated with his remark, with her mixed-up emotions and with him, Caitlin ignored his words. She wanted him to leave before she said or did something even more stupid than the treatment she'd just given him. Cavallo? Did she know the name? She had heard it somewhere before.

"What do I owe you?" he asked and took out his wallet.

She shook her head while she walked toward the door. "Nothing. I hope your back is better soon." He had to get out of her rooms, and quickly. She reached out to open the door, but his hand closed over hers and when she turned, he was standing right behind her.

"I have a question," he said.

"Yes?" She clutched the jamb, praying her knees wouldn't buckle. This close, he was even more overwhelming.

"The massage I've just been given, is that what you usually do?"

Her face flamed, but she ignored it and squared her shoulders. "You have a back problem. I tried to ease your pain. That's it."

"You haven't answered my question. Is that the usual treatment your patients get?"

"I…yes." She nodded and opened the door quickly. "I'm sorry if you didn't like it."

He smiled. This time her knees did buckle and she gripped the frame more firmly. His smile was devastating.

"I didn't say I didn't like it." He bent down till his face was centimeters from hers. "As you very well know, I liked it just fine," he said, his brown eyes dark.

She couldn't move and for endless moments they looked at one another. He pulled back and left, still smiling.

Her legs refused to move and like a lovesick puppy, she stared after him. He entered the lift and when he turned to press the button on the panel in front of him, she quickly closed the door and walked back to her desk. He'd thrown some notes down and she picked them up slowly. The amount was hopelessly too much. Her legs finally gave out completely and she sat down.

What was wrong with her? Yes, he was attractive and yes, she was a red-blooded female, but she'd never experienced this kind of reaction to a man. For one wild minute, she'd wanted to throw herself at him.

Because…okay, damn it, now that she was alone, she could admit it. He did something to her. She'd never been so turned on by a man's presence. It felt as if a part of her had been locked up, and around Don, needs and passions she'd been unaware of had been unleashed. Oh, damn it.

She grabbed her bag. Her sisters were waiting for her. She would have to try and pretend he'd been just another patient.

CHAPTER 3

"Okay, tell us about the hunk," Zoe said the minute Caitlin joined them.

"What hunk?" She tried for nonchalant, but Zoe pointed to her face.

"The one who had you all feverish," Zoe said.

"Why don't I know anything about a hunk?" Dana asked, leaning forward.

"I wasn't feverish. I don't know what gave you that idea," Caitlin said and grabbed the menu.

"You were blushing, your eyes were dilated—"

"Oh, nonsense. You were seeing things." Caitlin turned to Hannah, hoping to shift the attention away from herself.

Dana grabbed her arm. "What hunk? I'm your BFF! Why don't I know anything about a hunk in your life?"

Caitlin rolled her eyes. "There is no hunk in my life," she said, irritated. "I had a patient, that's it."

"A gorgeous patient, Dana. Jet black hair, brown eyes, and a very, very sexy body," Zoe insisted.

"Okay, the man is attractive, but he is a patient. I treated him during the Wines to Whales race last weekend. He has a house in Hermanus and came for another treatment today. I will probably never see him again. That's it."

She turned to Hannah. "I want to know why you became all snow-queenish when you asked about Don's brother. What was his name again?" Caitlin asked, hoping Zoe and Dana would switch their attention to Hannah.

Hannah frowned and picked up her cup. "His name is Darryn and I don't like him."

"But why? If he looks anything like his brother…" Zoe said.

"You do know who we are talking about here?" Hannah asked. "The Cavallos? Tycoon brothers who own I don't know how many boutique hotels here in South Africa and in the Seychelles."

"Ooh, nice. A hunk with money," sighed Zoe. "Sounds like a catch to me."

"Of course. That's why he looks so familiar. The papers are always filled with news about their hotels," Caitlin said, frowning. "You don't often see a picture of them, though."

"Yeah, they have a thing about their privacy. However, you'll find lots of interesting clips about them in the tabloids and on social media." Hannah grimaced. "The Cavallos love women. Note the plural, please. I don't think I've ever seen any one of them with the same woman on more than one occasion."

"I keep forgetting you're famous," Zoe said. "You mingle with all these people one reads about in the press. What I don't understand is why you haven't latched on to any one of them. If the rest of them look like their brother, they must all be gorgeous."

"No, thank you. Can we now please talk about something else?" Hannah asked, clearly irritated.

"So, there are two hunks? One for Hannah and one for Caitlin?" Dana asked, still frowning.

Hannah nearly choked on her coffee and quickly put her cup down. "I am definitely not interested in this hunk, as you call him. And if you go for that kind of look, there are actually four of them." Hannah pressed her lips together.

"Well, there you have it. Even if I were interested, which I'm not, he is completely out of my league. People like me simply don't mix with the likes of the Cavallos," Caitlin said.

"You can't be more right," Hannah agreed.

For a minute longer, Caitlin stared at Hannah. Something was bothering her sister. She would love to know why the usually calm and collected Hannah got upset about this guy, but she knew Hannah would only talk about it when she was ready. For now, the less they talked about the sexy brothers, the better for her.

The waiter appeared to take their order. The minute he left, Zoe started again.

"Okay, I'm sorry, but I have to know. Did anything happen between you and this Don? When you came out of the treatment room, you were blushing and your eyes were wild. Come on, you can tell us," she cajoled.

"Nothing happened. I just treated his back…"

"Is he as sexy under his clothes as he looks?" Zoe asked, giggling.

"Yes…no…I…don't know. I worked on his back," Caitlin said irritably. "Can we please change the subject?"

It was quiet for a moment.

"You like this Don," Dana said with a sly smile.

"I don't—"

"You totally like this guy," she repeated.

"I don't like this guy. I haven't said I like this guy!" Caitlin called out, frustration making her speak much louder than she normally would have.

Heads turned in their direction and she sighed.

She tried again. "I don't like him as in like him, but he's a client."

"Did he kiss you?" asked Zoe.

"No! What on earth gave you that idea? He didn't kiss

me! Who said he kissed me?"

"Oh, so you want him to kiss you?" Zoe asked, obviously trying to keep a straight face.

"I didn't say that! What is wrong with you? We…I…he…"

Hannah, who'd been silent so far, touched her hand. "I'd stay as far away as possible, if I were you. You must make up your own mind but remember that you've been warned."

"Relax, Hannah. There is nothing going on. He's a client. I treated his back. That's it. What is it with you and this Darryn?" She was fed up with her sisters' teasing.

"It's a long, boring story. Just keep your distance. The Cavallos are not to be trusted."

"Well, the chances that he and I will see one another ever again are non-existent. It's not as if we move in the same circles," she said drolly. "When are you going back to Cape Town?" Caitlin asked Hannah, hoping to talk about something else.

"Like I said, I'm flying to the Seychelles for a shoot sometime next week, so I thought I'd stay with Mum for a few days before I go back to my place in Clifton," said Hannah.

"Which reminds me. Mum said to ask you for lunch tomorrow," said Zoe. "You are also invited, Dana. She wants all her girls together for a change, and she wants to know what's going on in your love life." She grinned.

Caitlin groaned. "What did you tell her? You know what she's like. The minute she thinks there's a man on the horizon for any of us, she starts looking for wedding dresses and fairy lights."

"We didn't tell her anything. We only met your Don this afternoon, remember? We didn't know you were interested in anyone," Zoe said.

"I'm not interested in anyone, least of all—"

"A tall, sexy cyclist?" said Zoe, wiggling her eyebrows.

Hannah leaned forward. "`Now that I think about it,

Mum did mention that you talked about a cyclist."

"I didn't talk about a cyclist! She was the one who went on and on about the men in tight shorts…" Caitlin said hotly, but her sisters and Dana just giggled more.

***

When she finally got home, it was late and already dark. It had been nice to catch up with her sisters and Dana. Hannah mostly worked overseas, Zoe was forever racing between her interior decorating projects, and Dana's teaching kept her busy all hours of the day. They seldom had a chance to get together.

She got out of her car and looked up at the sky. And a pair of dark chocolate brown eyes appeared before her. Blinking furiously, she tried to think of everyday things, of her work, her patients, but vivid images of Don's muscled back, of her hands on his flesh, of his scent all around her, kept haunting her as she slipped inside her house.

And that smoldering look when he'd told her he couldn't get up would probably stay with her for the rest of her life. Nobody had ever looked at her in quite that way. She didn't want to think about the fact that he'd been as aroused as she'd been.

Aargh! She didn't trust men, remember? There was a whole blog out in cyberspace to attest to that. She didn't need Hannah's warning to know Don was no exception. He was rich, powerful, insanely attractive, and a celebrity to boot. There had to be millions of women falling for him. She didn't need to join *that* circus.

Besides, at twenty-nine she had very few illusions left about forever-after. Her own father had walked away from his wife and three daughters and the little she'd seen from her friends' marriages conveyed something she'd known all along: that the romance stories her mother wrote were just that. Stories. Fairytales.

Somehow, she would have to ignore this ridiculous

feeling. The man hadn't even touched her but he'd lit a fire inside of her the first time she'd touched him, one that wouldn't stop smoldering.

And he wasn't even Mister Nice Guy. On the contrary. So far, he'd mostly been surly and rude. Except for that last smile. Irritated with her thoughts, she started undressing.

Maybe next time Pete, or Steve, or whoever the dentist with rooms adjacent to hers was, called to ask her out on a date again, she'd accept. He was also quite attractive and maybe she'd find out that he didn't fall into any of her existing categories. Surely, there had to be at least one other man out there who could also heat her blood?

***

Don pulled his T-shirt over his head before he continued painting the wall. It was late evening and he wanted to finish before he went to bed. Ever since Caitlin had put her hands on him that afternoon, his whole body was still on fire. Even now, hours after her treatment, his abs tightened when he thought about her touch.

He couldn't remember ever being this turned on by a woman. And he hadn't even kissed her. But her hands on his back… He swore. Hell, he'd probably only imagined that the massage was much more than a usual physiotherapy treatment.

Maybe because of all the steamy dreams he'd been having over the last week, he'd experienced her treatment as more erotic than it had been. She was simply doing her job. To her, he was only another patient.

He was going to make a point this coming week of seeing his own physiotherapist in Cape Town. What he did not want was to lie down for another session with the sexy physiotherapist. Hopefully his back would be fine by next weekend.

His phone rang. It was Darryn.

"So what's your excuse?" he growled. "David and Dale have already phoned with all sorts of reasons as to why they couldn't help me this weekend."

Darryn laughed. "No, I don't have an excuse. I'll see you tomorrow. That's why I'm phoning. I'm going to cycle to Hermanus, so I'll probably only see you later in the morning."

Don laughed. "It's fine. I'm joking. I really appreciate your help. You don't have to do this."

"Yeah, we do. So now you owe us," Darryn teased.

"I should have known." Don smiled. "By the way, I met a stunner this afternoon who knows you. Hannah Sutherland?"

Darryn swore.

Don chuckled. "Wow. She didn't use those exact words, but she's clearly not enamored with you, either. What happened?"

"Where did you meet her?" asked Darryn in a clipped voice.

"I…I went to see the physiotherapist who treated me last weekend again. Here, at her rooms in Hermanus. You know, the one from the tent? Anyway, I was too busy during the week to get to my own physiotherapist, and my back had been acting up again. If you remember, her name is Caitlin Sutherland. Well, Hannah is her sister. I met Hannah as I was leaving. Zoe, apparently another sister, was also there."

Darryn was silent for a moment. "I didn't really catch her surname. A pity. I liked the physio. Like Hannah, she's beautiful and sexy as hell. But if she and this Zoe are anything like their model sister, you should steer clear of her."

"Why? What happened?"

"Nothing I want to talk about. I'll see you tomorrow."

Don stared at his cell phone for a moment. Obviously something had happened between his brother and the model. But if Darryn didn't want to talk about it, so be it.

He had enough problems of his own.

The Sutherland sisters were beautiful and sexy. All three of them. Why, then, did he remember only one of them so vividly?

He swore again and dipped the brush in the paint. Caitlin was gorgeous, there was no doubt about it. But he didn't like the way his body took over his brain when she was in the vicinity. He didn't like the way his heart seemed to skip several beats when he so much as caught a glimpse of her. And he definitely didn't like the way the blood left his head and pooled down way below his middle. Hell, the last time he'd had such lustful thoughts about a girl was when he'd still been in high school.

Like any red-blooded male, he found women fascinating, but he had always been a bit wary around them and had never quite been able to work out what they really wanted. After he'd become successful, women were eager for his company, but he'd quickly realized that they were more interested in his money than in him.

He rarely had to make the effort to get to know a woman, as there always seemed to be one hanging on his arm. His experience with women had left him cynical, he knew, but he had yet to meet one who wasn't more interested in his money than in him.

He was thirty-three, he loved his job, enjoyed his hobbies, and was simply not interested in being just an ATM for someone. His mum kept telling them they needed wives, but so far, marriage had been something he'd steered clear of.

His parents had been married for forty years and as far as he could tell, they still loved each other and loved to spend time together. But what he admired most about them was the fact that they still talked to one another, argued about things, got excited about anything new, after all these years. He loved the way his mum's face still lit up when his dad entered a room and the way his dad's face softened when he saw his wife.

But he'd also seen how very seldom that happened in life. Too often, he looked at his married friends and saw disillusionment, a kind of weary resignation to the situation they found themselves in. That was not what he wanted. That was not the way he planned to spend the rest of his life.

He hadn't met a woman yet who could stir more than a mild interest, one who wasn't only interested in his position and money. But this physiotherapist...she obviously hadn't recognized him so far. But that would have changed by now. Her sister clearly knew enough to make the connection and know he had money.

He wasn't quite sure what to make of Caitlin. Something told him that she was the kind of woman who'd take over your mind, body, and soul. One who'd have you think of white picket fences, Labrador dogs, and kids before you'd realized what had hit you.

Don nearly dropped the paintbrush. Where the hell had that thought come from? He wasn't ready for settling down. Least of all with someone who was so opinionated. Yes, she was stunningly beautiful, but damn it, she had an opinion about everything.

Maybe it was time to spend time with another woman, have sex with her. No doubt the only reason his hormones went haywire after a simple massage was the fact that he hadn't been with a woman for some time.

He went through the list of women he knew. At this moment, nobody else seemed even mildly interesting, but surely if he thought long and hard, he could find someone to spend a nice evening with.

CHAPTER 4

Don tried to listen to Liz. He really did. He had realized too late why he'd stopped seeing her. She never stopped talking. Not even when she was eating. And she kept talking about his hotels, and money.

And to make matters worse, his gaze kept moving in another direction. They'd just sat down when the hairs on his arms had risen. He'd looked up and seen Caitlin sitting down at a table across the room. Of course there had always been the possibility that he would run into her at some point in Hermanus. He had a house here and liked to spend as much time as his work allowed in the little village. She lived and worked in the town. But he never thought it would actually happen.

His brothers had been available to help him during the previous weekend, and they had finished another bedroom. He could, of course, just hire someone to do the work, but they all enjoyed the physical labor. For them, it was also a way to relax, away from the public eye.

But even all the hard work couldn't stop him from thinking about the sexy physiotherapist. And he'd been thinking about her constantly. So when he'd bumped into Liz, he'd invited her for dinner. Spending an evening with her had seemed like a good idea at the time.

How the hell was he supposed to know that the smiling blond idiot Caitlin was with would pick the same date and venue he'd decided on when he took Liz out? And who was this guy? The thought she might have a boyfriend simply hadn't crossed his mind.

As if it moved of its own volition, he turned his head again. The guy Caitlin was with had now moved his chair and was sitting almost on top of her. He'd put his arm around her shoulders and was whispering in her ear. What the hell? Was that the kind of man she went for?

Caitlin saw him for the first time since she'd sat down. For a split second, his gaze met hers before her date put a hand under her chin and turned her head back to him.

Don felt like getting up and ramming his fist down the man's throat. He swallowed down his irritation. He was with another woman; he should be paying attention to her. He looked at Liz and nearly sighed aloud. It was not working.

Being with another woman hadn't helped. Even before he'd seen her in the restaurant, he hadn't been able to get Caitlin out of his head.

Again, he tried to focus on what Liz was saying. He glanced at his watch and nearly groaned out loud. They'd only been in the restaurant for an hour. How the hell was he going to survive listening to Liz prattling on and on for another couple of hours?

***

Caitlin took Pete's wandering hand in both of hers and removed it from her leg. She moved her chair slightly away from him.

It was not difficult to decide in which category the dentist would fall. The wandering-hands guy. Well, it was her own fault. She'd wanted to go out with a man, any man. So when Pete had wiggled his eyebrows at her and asked her out again, she'd agreed. She should have known a man who did that would be a bad date.

And to make a bad evening worse, she'd just seen Don Cavallo. With a blonde. In the same restaurant. What were the chances of that happening? She had assumed that the Cavallos would frequent one of Cape Town's many famous restaurants and would never have thought that she would run into him in a restaurant in this little village.

Pete moved closer again and she grabbed her bag.

"I have to powder my nose." She smiled and jumped up. As quickly as she could, she walked to the bathroom and closed the door behind her with a sigh of relief. Pete's aftershave or whatever he was wearing was sweet and suffocating, his hands cold, and his touch plain creepy. She walked to the nearest washbasin and splashed some of the cool water over her arms. Her face looked pale in the mirror.

The whole evening was a disaster, and completely pointless. She was out on a date with one man so that she could stop thinking about another one. But it wasn't working. Since she'd seen Don two weeks before, he had been constantly on her mind and in every one of her very steamy dreams.

And now she had at least another hour to kill before she could politely go home. She'd insisted, as she always did when she went out on a date, on meeting Pete here and was now very grateful that he didn't know where she lived and that she could drive off when she wanted to.

She opened the bathroom door and walked straight into what felt like a brick wall. Strong hands folded over her arms and instinctively she knew it was Don. Resigned, she looked up.

"Hi," she said.

"Hi," he answered, his expression closed.

She tried to extricate herself from his hold, but his hands moved farther down her arms and tightened. Her skin felt hot where his hands touched her.

"I didn't know you had a boyfriend," he said.

"He's not…he's not my boyfriend," she stammered before she could think and again tried to move away. This time, he took her hands in his. She shivered. When she looked up, he was smiling.

"I think we should…" he began but someone bumped into her back and she stepped aside. Her hands slid out of his and without looking at him again, she slipped past him.

"Did you see who that was?" someone whispered behind her. "It's Don Cavallo, the hotel tycoon."

Caitlin hurried back to her table. Her heart was hammering so loudly she was amazed no one else seemed to hear. What did Don want to tell her? They should what? Why would he even talk to her? She was from such a different world than the one he inhabited, they could have nothing in common.

Pete was on his cell phone as she approached the table. He smiled at her but continued talking. While she'd been in the bathroom, the waiter had brought their food. She sipped from her wine while he kept on talking.

She could smell Don on her hand. His scent was totally different from Pete's. There was a whiff of sandalwood, mixed with a touch of citrus and even a dash of thyme, if she wasn't mistaken. Whatever it was, it was all male and very, very sexy.

Her fingers weren't steady as she put the glass down and looked at Pete again. He was merrily chatting away on his phone.

She waited for another minute before she picked up her knife and fork. She'd had a busy day and had skipped lunch. If nothing else, she was at least going to get a meal out of this miserable night.

***

Caitlin stepped from the restaurant to the pavement and inhaled the fresh sea air. Thank heavens she'd managed to escape. She rummaged in her bag for her car keys. Pete had been on the phone for most of the evening and during the times he hadn't been talking to someone, he'd pounce on her. His arms would snake out, he'd drag her closer to him, and then he would try to nuzzle her neck. Not a technique that worked for her.

She'd been trying to leave politely when his phone rang again. He held his finger up to silence her and answered his cell phone. At that point she'd given up pretending she was enjoying the evening. She'd left. He'd called her back while covering the mouthpiece of his phone. It had not been difficult to ignore him.

Her own phone rang while she was crossing the road.

"How was your date with the dentist?" Zoe asked.

"Horrible. Probably the worst date I've ever been on," she grumbled and walked faster when she saw her car. Living in South Africa meant being vigilant at all times. But the parking lot was clear: a guard was standing nearby. "The only good thing about the evening is that I now have plenty to write about."

"So, in which category will he fall?"

"Several, I think. He'll fit into wandering-hands guy, but I now have a whole new category to write about. Guy-who-talks-on-his-cell-during-a-date category."

Zoe laughed. "Well, now you know. Forget about him. What about that sexy cyclist we saw at your rooms? He is so gorgeous."

"Let me think," she said, then didn't bother to hide the sarcasm in her voice. "Maybe because he isn't merely another cyclist. Remember, we're talking about the rich and famous, not our regular kind of date. Anyway, from what I've seen tonight, he has a girlfriend."

"Why? Did you see him?"

"Yes, in the same restaurant. With a blonde, so I don't think he's on the market."

"Really?"

"Zoe, seriously. I'm not looking for a man. I'm quite

happy as I am."

Zoe giggled. "All I know is that the air around you two sizzles."

"I don't know what you're talking about…" Caitlin began, just as she caught a movement at her side. The guard?

"Got to go," she said and quickly turned, her car keys ready in her hand. Beware the poor sod that wanted to bother her that night. At this point in the evening she was in a fighting mood.

But it was Don who stood there, hands in his pockets. The streetlights were bright enough for her to see him clearly.

She dropped her hands from their halfway-up position. Oh hell, what had he heard? He came closer. She swallowed.

"Where's your girlfriend?" was the first thing that popped out of her mouth. Caitlin nearly groaned out load. She looked away and unlocked her car. "Sorry, none of my business," she mumbled and opened the door.

"She's just a friend."

"Did you enjoy your date?" she asked.

He shook his head. "I was watching you the whole night."

Stunned, she swallowed.

"And you? Did you have a nice time?" he asked.

"I…" At a complete loss, she frantically tried to think of a word, any word. Nothing came to mind. She shook her head. *He's been watching me all night?*

He stepped around so the car door was between them. Her hands were resting lightly on the door, her fingers tingling. She vividly remembered how it had felt to touch him.

"Thought so." His smile was devastating. "I'd like to take you out, Caitlin."

"As in a date?" she asked, still stunned.

"Yes, Caitlin, as in a date." He touched her cheek.

"There is something here," he said, and then motioned with his hand between them.

She didn't move, just stared at him. Was he really asking her out on a date?

"I don't know what it is, but it's keeping me awake at night. Let's try a date and see how we like it. Friday around seven?" he asked. "I'll pick you up and we'll have dinner."

Caitlin stared at him for another minute before she was sure she could string a few words together. "Don, you…me…" She shook her head and grimaced. "We live in two completely different worlds; we have nothing in common. You are…you, the papers are full of your businesses. I'm a physiotherapist from Hermanus. I don't think—"

"Then don't. Think, that is." He smiled. "You do know that you can't believe everything you read in the papers. And I happen to like this physiotherapist from Hermanus."

She looked at him a moment longer. This was so not what she should be doing. Hannah's warning and her own misgivings about him swirled around in her head.

His gaze never left hers.

She was a big girl. And if she prepared herself for the worst, then surely she'd be fine.

"Where? I'll meet you—"

"I'll pick you up," he said and lowered his head.

"You don't know where I live and I always drive myself," she managed just before his lips touched hers lightly.

She was speechless for the second time within a few seconds and her breath hitched in her throat. Her lips opened and his tongue dove in.

His hands folded over hers and except for his mouth, he wasn't touching her anywhere else. But with just that contact he nearly had her whimpering and begging for more.

Wow, this guy knew how to kiss, was the last coherent

thought she had time for. Then a torrent simply picked her up and dragged her along. His lips were warm, wet, and unrelenting. She was unable to do anything else but kiss him back.

After hours, minutes, seconds had passed, a car horn hooted nearby and he lifted his head slowly, his hands still covering hers.

"You can't kiss me. I don't know you," she whispered and realized immediately how ridiculous it sounded.

He just lifted an eyebrow and stared at her mouth.

Muttering, she got into her car and tried to close the door. She had to get away from this guy. His presence alone made her behave in ways that she wouldn't have thought possible. What was wrong with her?

Don closed the door and bent down. "Friday night," he said, and put a finger on her lips.

Before she could do anything, he'd stepped back.

In a daze, she drove away. Just before she turned to the right, she looked in her rearview mirror. Don was standing where she'd left him, looking after her.

It was only while she was parking her car in her garage, that she realized she'd been smiling idiotically all the way from the restaurant.

CHAPTER 5

Caitlin's phone rang just as she was finishing her run. Still a little out of breath, she answered.

"Why do you sound so out of breath?" Dana wanted to know. "Anything going on that I should know about?"

Caitlin sighed. "No, Dana, I've been for a run."

"You haven't answered my other question. Anything going on that I should know about? You don't maybe have a date with a certain hunk?"

"How on earth did you know?" Caitlin asked with a groan.

Dana laughed. "I didn't. You've just told me! I knew it. There was just something about your voice when you spoke about him. I knew something was going on. So, where is he taking you and what are you going to wear?"

"I don't know and I don't know. It's just a date. We met by accident in a parking lot and he asked me out. It's no big deal."

"Mmm, you forget I know you well. But okay, I won't ask for more details. Except, what are you going to wear?"

Caitlin sighed. "I don't know. It's probably just a dinner. It's not as if Hermanus has that much of a nightlife."

37

"Well, maybe next time he'll take you to a fancy club in Cape Town."

"There won't be a next time, Dana. This is a one-off. I'll probably never see him again after Friday night. Remember who he is and who I am."

"You're a beautiful woman, that's who you are and—"

"Oh, Dana, you know what I mean. He lives in a complete other world where money is never an issue. I simply don't know how to talk to people like that."

"People like that?" Dana giggled. "You sound like a snob!"

"I mean people like me have nothing to say to people like him," Caitlin tried again.

"Still sounds snobbish to me, but okay. So, the date is on Friday?"

"Yes, the date is on Friday, but don't—"

"Bye, got to go," Dana interrupted her.

"...tell my mother or sisters." Caitlin finished her sentence even though she knew no one was listening.

She shook her head. It was difficult for her to put what she was feeling into words. She didn't understand the excitement, the strange longing inside of her, so how could she explain her feelings to anyone else?

At the same time, she couldn't help but feel that a date with the handsome Cavallo would be a huge mistake. And to argue the circles they moved in were just too different for any kind of relationship between them to work? That wasn't snobbish, just realistic.

***

Caitlin froze. That couldn't be the front doorbell, could it? She looked at the time on her phone. It was too early. He'd said seven o'clock, she was sure of it. She looked around frantically. Her whole bed was covered with discarded outfits. Her hair was still a mess and she hadn't finished her makeup.

The bell rang again and she heard her mother's voice. She groaned out loud but stormed down the corridor and flung open the front door.

"Mother, what are you doing here?" Caitlin didn't even try to keep the irritation out of her voice.

"Hello, darling, I love you too." Her mother smiled and held up a bag. "I bought something nice for you and wanted to drop it off."

Her mother walked past her and Caitlin closed the door. "Thank you, but I have enough clothes. And we both know the clothes are not the reason you're here. Dana told you that I'm going on a date and you want to meet the guy."

Her mother turned to face her, trying to look apologetic and failing miserably. She laughed. "I know and I'm sorry, but I'm so excited and I'm dying to meet this hunk Zoe talks about. He was the only topic of conversation last Sunday. This is going to be such a lovely story. Do you know where…?"

Caitlin stopped listening and resignedly walked back to her room. Maybe it was a good idea for Don to meet her mother now. Maybe he'd run away screaming even before their date could begin.

"Well, it's a good thing I've bought something new for you. You obviously don't have anything to wear," her mother said as she followed her into her room and stared at the pile of clothes on her bed.

"I have enough clothes, Mum, I just haven't decided yet what to wear."

"Well, try this on," her mother said and pulled a tiny scrap of material out of the shopping bag. She shook it and held it up.

"With those black skinny jeans you wore last Sunday it will be perfect. Oooh and these shoes," she said, picking up a discarded pair of blue heels. "They're so sexy. Come on, try on the top, you know you want to." Her mother held out the garment.

Caitlin sighed and took it from her mother. The top was perfect, exactly what she'd been looking for. It was a frilly boob-tube that would leave her shoulders bare. The blue color was the hue she loved and the style, her favorite. It was the beginning of October and the evenings were still cool but she had a jacket she could take with her.

She slipped it over her head. Of course, it fit perfectly. "Thanks, Mum," she said and smiled for the first time. "I love it." She pulled on the jeans and turned to the mirror.

"You look beautiful. But then, you always do," her mother said. "Sit down and let me comb your hair."

"I thought I'd put it in a ponytail—" she began, but her mother shook her head adamantly.

"No, you won't. You have gorgeous hair. You are not going to pin it up." She motioned toward the chair. "In my stories, the hero must be able to run his fingers through the heroine's hair. How can he do that if it's pinned up? Come on, sit down."

"Mum, we're going on a date. A first date. No fingers involved," she said, trying hard not to think about Don's big hand covering hers.

***

The woman who opened the door wasn't Caitlin. She was an older, smiling version.

"You must be Don." She stepped back. "Come in. Caitlin is on her way."

He heard a sound to his right and turned. And there she was. His heart stopped and he couldn't breathe. The air around him was too thick, too loaded, too dense.

"Hi, Don." Caitlin smiled and he exhaled slowly.

She was exquisitely beautiful. The blue top she was wearing lovingly embraced each generous curve and the sight of her bare shoulders left him nearly salivating.

He should say something. He opened his mouth to speak but for a moment he was unable to form one coherent word. Clearing his throat, he tried again.

"You look stunning," he said, touching her hand. A flowery scent stole around him and he felt lightheaded.

She smiled again and turned to her mum. This time he nearly swallowed his tongue whole. A pair of tight-fitting jeans stretched neatly over a very sexy bottom. Oh man, was he in trouble. The evening had not begun yet, the mother was still here, and all he could think about was having this woman under him, his fingers tangled in her hair.

"Mum, this is Don Cavallo. Don, my mother, Brenda."

Reluctantly, he tore his eyes away from Caitlin and shook the older woman's hand.

"So, Don, tell me, are you an only child?" her mother asked, eyes twinkling.

"No, I have three brothers," he said, trying to behave normally.

"Oh really. And where are they? What do they do? Are your parents still alive? Come, sit down and tell me." Caitlin's mother turned for the matched, plush chairs nearby.

"Mum, really, now is not the time for a family tree," Caitlin said and gave him an apologetic look.

"It's fine. I like talking about my family." Don smiled and took a seat opposite her mother. "My brothers and I work together. Dale, Darryn, and David joined the business about two years ago. After their studies they all pursued their dreams, but we've found a way to use all of their skills. Dale is an architect, so he's involved with new developments. Darryn majored in Economics but photography is his passion, so he takes care of marketing, and David used to be a journalist. He works closely with Darryn. We all live in and around Cape Town."

"All your names start with a D?"

Don smiled. "Yes, our mum said it was easier for her. This way, even if she mixes up our names, the first part will be correct."

"And your parents?" asked Caitlin's mother again.

"My parents are alive and well. They live in Rondebosch. My dad is a psychiatrist and works from home. And my mum has her own restaurant, Rosa's in Cape Town for the past, I don't know, probably thirty years."

Caitlin's mum clapped her hands. "I love that place!" she exclaimed. "And I love the food! I don't know what I did wrong, but my girls can't cook—"

Caitlin took her mother's arms and pulled her up. "Mum, we have to go. Come on, I'll walk you out."

"I can wait up for you," the older woman said.

"Goodnight, Mum. Thanks for stopping by," Caitlin said while pulling her mother toward the door.

Her mother smiled at him. "I'm so glad you've finally asked Caitlin on a date. From the first time she spoke about you—"

"Mum!" exclaimed Caitlin and opened the door. "We have to go."

"You must all come for dinner," Caitlin's mother called over her shoulder.

The two women walked to the other car parked in the driveway. Don was glad for the moment alone. *Wow, so now Catlin's mother knows everything there is to know about my family.* He inhaled some fresh air, hoping to clear his head.

The minute he'd laid eyes on Caitlin, every one of his senses went into overdrive. He was aware of her, of her scent, of her body, all his feelings on high alert. Somewhere inside of him an ache had opened up. He wasn't sure why, or what it was: all he knew for certain was that there was no other place he'd rather be than here, with her.

Over the past week, he'd tried to get on with his life, tried to keep his brain busy with work stuff. He was out on his bike early every morning, trying to tire himself out so that he could fall into a dreamless sleep just one night. But it didn't help.

It didn't matter where he was or what he was doing. In the middle of a meeting, on the plane on his way to one of their hotels, or while cycling early in the morning, thoughts about her would intrude, and disrupt his days. And nights.

He'd woken up hard and ready for her each morning. He hadn't had so many cold showers since puberty.

Up until now, the business had been the most important part of his life. Within a few weeks, one sexy physiotherapist had changed all that. And he wasn't sure he was very comfortable with the idea she could so completely take over his thoughts.

She waved to her mother and smiled as she walked back to him. "I'm sorry about my mother. She is an incurable romantic and is always trying to find men for her three daughters. But don't worry, I'm not looking. Let me just get my bag and lock the door, then we can go."

She walked past him and he caught another hint of flowers. Without conscious thought, he followed her and closed the door behind him.

"Don't close the door—"

That was as far as she got. "I haven't been looking either," he murmured before he pulled her close and kissed her.

She was a perfect fit. She tried to say something, but when her lips parted, he slipped his tongue inside. Her arms locked around his neck and she melted against him. Instantly, he was hard as rock.

He gathered her close, pressing himself against her. A kiss. That was all he wanted, all he'd been wanting for days. A kiss was supposed to be simple. It was something people did regularly. He'd hoped that it would ease the strange ache he had inside of him. But there was nothing simple or regular about kissing Caitlin Sutherland. And the ache wasn't eased.

He skimmed his hands down her sides, then up again and this time the backs of his hands touched her breasts. He swallowed her moan and cupped them. Beneath his fingers, her heart tripped and his own skipped a beat.

She was burning up. Any minute now she'd be going up in flames. Without taking her lips from his, Caitlin pressed her hands against Don's shoulders. He lifted his head. His breath was ragged, his eyes molten chocolate.

"Do you want to go out?" he asked.

Caitlin started shaking her head, but then reason took over and she stepped back.

"Don, no…I don't know you and we…that is, you said…" She tried to smile. "Let's have dinner."

He stared at her for another minute before he took her hand. "Okay, let's have dinner. I'll tell you everything you want to know about me. But, Caitlin," he said as he brushed his fingers over her lips, "next time I kiss you, you won't want to stop me again."

Her knees wobbled and she nodded. Speech was completely beyond her.

CHAPTER 6

They were halfway through their dinner when Caitlin realized that they hadn't stopped talking for one minute. There had been no awkward silences, no frantic thinking to find something to talk about; they'd moved from one topic to the next with the ease of old friends. Except friendly was not how she would describe what she was feeling.

He had asked her about her work and had actually listened when she spoke. And, true to his promise, he had told her about himself. If only the basics: where he grew up, where he went to school, where he studied. But different to most other men she'd been out with, he didn't volunteer any major accomplishments. She had to ask a lot of questions before she found out that he had a master's degree in Economics.

At this point of the evening it was also clear that she had no group on her blog into which Don Cavallo could be filed; he was a category all on his own. Nice guy didn't quite describe him, nor did sexy guy. He was so much more than just words.

Caitlin put her fork down. Wow. Where had that thought come from? She lifted her glass to her mouth and when she swallowed, her eyes met Don's. He had been saying something but when their gazes met, he stopped talking.

"Something wrong?" he asked.

Caitlin could only shake her head. Because she was very worried that if she were to open her mouth, it would be to say something stupid like *I'm having a wonderful time and I want to touch you.*

But he had to have read something in her eyes, because the next minute he threw down his serviette, then some notes on the table, and grabbed her hand. She just had time to snatch her handbag.

"Don, what is going on?" she asked, nearly running in an effort to keep up with his long strides.

Outside the restaurant he took a breath before he looked down at her. "You look at me like that in a room full of people…" he began, but someone laughed out loud near them, drowning out the rest of his words. Cussing softly, he pulled her closer to him and with his arm around her shoulders, steered her toward his car. "You make it very difficult for me to keep my hands to myself," he said curtly.

Wordlessly, he helped her into the car and walked around to the driver's side. She gulped in some air. Oh boy, she was in so much trouble. He even opened and closed the car door for her. She couldn't remember the last time a date did that. She was a modern woman who could do things for herself but being with someone who made her feel so cherished was a heady feeling.

And then he was sitting next to her, closing the door on his side. The big sports car was suddenly too small. She swallowed and crossed her arms. Every nerve in her body was tingling, all her senses were on alert.

When they left the parking area, Don took her hand and stepped on the pedal. His hand was big and warm. His thumb moved restlessly up and down her palm, igniting tiny flames just below her skin.

Neither of them spoke. The air became dense, making breathing nearly impossible. Caitlin moved restlessly. It was too much. The feeling, the heat, Don's presence. Way too much.

After what felt like ages, they reached her house. He jumped out and this time she didn't wait for him to open her door. She got out, frantically looking for the keys of the front door. She found them just as he reached her side.

Without looking at him, she walked up the steps to the door. By this time, her whole body was shivering. Anticipation, longing, craving—all these feelings curling up inside of her left her incapable of any rational thought. She tried to put the key in the lock but it fell from her trembling fingers. Don picked it up, unlocked the door, and pushed her inside. And then she was in his arms, his mouth on hers.

There was a roaring in his ears that blotted out everything else. He was only aware of Caitlin. All he could smell was her rose fragrance, all he could hear were the sounds coming from her throat, all he could feel was her soft skin under his fingers. She was all that mattered.

Their tongues met, started a slow dance. She tasted like no one else. His hands skimmed over her naked shoulders, down her sides, then slipped underneath her top. Her skin was soft. Like petals. His hands journeyed upward, molding the contours of her body, discovering all the places that made her catch her breath.

Finally, he could fold his hand over the softness of her breast, and she melted. He teased her nipples into rock-hard beads and swallowed her whimper. His whole being was focused on pleasuring her, on showing her how incredibly sexy he found her, how beautiful she was.

Her fingers fisted his shirt and with a soft oath he quickly pulled it over his head. She gulped in some air and with a slight smile trailed her fingers over his torso, further stimulating his already heightened senses. Her lips were swollen from his kisses, her eyes heavy and dark.

With a groan, he captured her mouth again. Her hands were tangled in his hair and she was urging him on with her fingers. Impatiently, he tugged her top down and her breasts sprang free.

"Beautiful. You're so beautiful," he breathed before he bent down again and took a nipple into his mouth.

Her body moved into his, her arms surrounded him, and he was oblivious to anything else. He caressed and suckled, teased and pleasured, first the one breast, then the other, until he was burning up inside.

"Don," she moaned restlessly and moved against him.

His hands glided down her sides. Damn, she was wearing a pair of jeans. He had to touch her, had to feel her heat. His hand cupped her through the denim and her broken moan nearly brought him to his knees.

Trying to get oxygen into his lungs, he lifted his head.

"If we don't stop now, I won't be able to," he growled and pulled her close to him so that they were skin against skin.

Unfocused, she just stared up at him. He bent his head to kiss her again but his phone rang.

Caitlin blinked and tried to figure out where she was. She had been swept away in a torrent of sensation, the likes of which she had never experienced before in her life. It was difficult to suddenly do ordinary things like deciding where she was or make conversation.

With a curse, Don took his phone out of the pocket of his pants. "Yes," he barked, then caressed her cheek before he walked away.

Caitlin looked down at herself. Her breasts were free, still tingling from Don's touch and her nipples were pointing cheekily upward as if asking for more attention. With a mortified groan, she pulled up her top. She had never before allowed a man to touch her this way on a first date.

She folded her arms around herself. She wanted this man with an intensity that scared her. If his cell phone hadn't rung, she'd have dragged him to her bed without a second thought. Her body was throbbing everywhere he had touched her.

He turned around and put his phone back in his pocket. He picked up his shirt and threw it over his head.

"I have to go." He drew her closer. "Something came up." For a minute longer he held her, then stepped away.

"This isn't over. I'm not sure when I'll be able to talk to you again, but we haven't finished." Before he opened the front door, he bent down. The kiss left her clutching the door.

It was only much later, after the sound of his car had long since disappeared, that she was able to move.

***

Her phone rang early. She was instantly awake and grabbed it, full of anticipation. Her dreams had been filled with steamy scenes in which Don had been the main star. Her body was singing as if his hands had just been exploring every centimeter of her skin.

But it was her mother, not Don.

"Hi, Mum," she said, sitting up against the pillows. She wasn't disappointed, she told herself. She had known she probably wouldn't hear from him again even though he did say they weren't finished, whatever that meant.

"And? Is he still there?" her mother asked, clearly delighted with the possibility.

"Mum, no!" she called out. "It was a first date, remember?" She blushingly closed her eyes. Her mother definitely didn't need to know the details of this particular first date.

"Well, I saw the way he was looking at you, my dear, and that man had much more on his mind than just a meal."

"Well, nothing happened. We had dinner, he left, I went to bed alone."

"Oh well, if you don't like him—"

"I haven't said I don't like him—" Caitlin said.

"Oh, so you do like him?" her mother teased.

Caitlin sighed. "Mum, yes, I like him, but we don't move in the same circles. I will probably never see him again."

"Well, that's a pity. He looks like a really nice man. But, if you've decided it won't work, that's that. Anyway, why I'm also calling is to find out whether you've heard from Hannah?"

"Well, she phoned me from the airport on Wednesday on her way to the Seychelles, but I haven't heard from her again. It's only been three days, Mum."

"I know, but I'm concerned. It's not like her not to call or send an email."

"I'm sure she's fine, Mum. She's on an island, busy with a shoot. As you know by now, she usually has a crazy schedule."

"You're right. I know you're right. I'll stop worrying."

Caitlin laughed. "Try, Mum, and start with another story. That usually keeps you busy." She smiled.

"Yeah, yeah, and out of your hair," her mother grumbled. "I still think your Don is very sexy."

"Mum!" Caitlin laughed.

"What? I'm not too old to know when a man is sexy. And this one is very sexy."

"Goodbye, Mum." Caitlin smiled and put the phone down while her mother was still talking about Don.

She looked at her watch. It was time to get up. And time to put any thoughts about Don Cavallo out of her head. She touched her lips. The man could kiss. Wow. And make her feel things she thought were only possible between the pages of her mother's books.

But this was real life and romantic interludes like last night were probably only meant to be few and far between.

Even though she would never see him again, at least she now knew what was possible when you kissed the right man. She jumped out of bed, groaning as she gave her sides a stretch. He was so not the right man for her and the sooner she accepted that he was not going to phone, the sooner she could move on with her life.

***

Don't trust men. Period. Even if he looks like a Greek god, don't believe a word he says. "I'll phone you" is just his way of saying goodbye. Even if he kisses you like you've never been kissed before, don't fall for it—he will not phone, you will never hear from him again. Maybe it's the way they're wired; I don't know. But be warned. Don't trust men!

Feeling even more grumpy than she had when she'd walked into her rooms that morning, Caitlin reread the last paragraph of what she'd just written on her blog. She'd spent an entire weekend staring at her phone even though she'd known all along what she'd just written. He was not going to phone.

She just had to try and get rid of her frustration in some way. Her usual morning run hadn't done the trick, so she'd hoped that if she shared her irritation of the whole sitting-in-front-of-the-phone-and-hoping-he'd-call with the virtual world, she might get over Don and feel better. But now she only felt worse. She should just delete the whole thing.

Before she could touch the keyboard, though, Maggie stormed through the door, a newspaper in her hand.

"Caitlin, look," she said and pointed at a picture in the paper. "This is Don Cavallo with some beauty queen on his arm as usual. I felt so miserable that Friday when he made an appointment to see you, I didn't realize he was *the* Don Cavallo. And I've never asked you about that late Friday afternoon appointment I made. But it was him, wasn't it?" she asked and pushed the paper under Caitlin's nose.

Caitlin froze when she heard Don's name. Like a robot, she took the paper and looked down. It was Don, all right. And yes, the beautiful woman hanging on his arm was probably a beauty queen. A big hole opened up inside of her.

"It was taken at the airport. I wonder where they were going. Paris? London? Prague? An exotic island? It doesn't say." Maggie sighed.

Caitlin threw the paper down. "Yes, that is Mr. Cavallo and he was my patient for one afternoon. And their whereabouts, Maggie, are not our problem. What time is our first appointment?" she asked, trying to listen to what Maggie was saying while a thousand thoughts raced through her head. Why? Why would he kiss her like that and touch her like that if he had a girlfriend? Why say he'd phone her if he had no intention of doing that?

The phone rang and Maggie answered. Caitlin walked to her own desk and sat down.

She should have known. He was, after all, a man. Even her own father hadn't been able to stay faithful to his wife, the mother of his children. A dull ache formed just below her heart. She grimaced. There was a category for Don Cavallo, after all. He would fit nicely into the cheating-lying-bastard one.

Maggie called her name and held out the phone to her.

"One of your sisters, I think," she said.

Caitlin stood up and took the phone. Strange. Her sisters normally phoned her on her cell.

"Hello," she said.

"Caitlin?" a soft voice asked.

An ice-cold fist clenched her insides. "Hannah? Yes, it's me. What's wrong?" She clutched the phone

"…cell phone lost…accident…hit-and-run…hospital," were the only words that registered.

CHAPTER 7

Why the hell didn't she answer her phone? Don maneuvered his car through the traffic. He'd been in meetings since he'd set foot in Johannesburg on Friday night. The kitchen staff in two of their hotels had gone on strike and they'd spent the entire weekend and the whole of yesterday trying to come to a mutual agreement.

He was so tired but he wanted to get back to Caitlin as soon as possible. He remembered he'd mentioned the fact he probably wouldn't have time to call; he knew how chaotic these kinds of talks could be. But the minute he finished, he'd tried to phone her. However, since yesterday afternoon, her phone had been and still was switched off, apparently. He didn't want to leave a message and was anxious to hear her voice.

Thoughts of her had been the only thing that kept him sane over the past few days. He hadn't thought this whole mess would take so long to sort out, but he also knew that it wouldn't help to rush discussions. They had always prided themselves on the fact that they paid their workers well and kept them happy. But something or someone had to have spooked them and false rumors had spread. It had taken them nearly three whole days to undo the mischief-making.

And now all he wanted was to get back to Caitlin. He had been so frustrated on Friday night when Darryn had called about the trouble. The last thing he had wanted to do was to leave the sexy woman he had in his arms.

He had to have the number of her rooms somewhere, he remembered, and asked for the number on the system of his car. When he heard the dial tone, he sighed with relief. Even if she was busy, he'd hopefully be able to speak to her receptionist.

"Caitlin Sutherland's rooms, good afternoon," a voice sang over the phone.

"Hi, this is Don Cavallo—"

"Mr. Cavallo," she gushed, "we saw your photo in the newspaper!"

Don did a double take. He didn't know anything about a photo in the newspaper. They had tried to keep the whole business out of the papers. Why would there be a photograph of him in a paper?

"What paper?" he asked.

The voice giggled and mentioned the name of a tabloid paper he couldn't stand. "You were with that beauty queen...I showed it to Caitlin as well. She—"

"May I please speak to Caitlin?" he asked, not bothering to hide his irritation with the voice on the other side of the line. He vaguely remembered the woman who'd greeted him at the Johannesburg airport and now that he thought about it, there had been a camera around, but he hadn't thought of it again. What Caitlin had to be thinking was not hard to guess.

"She's not here. She's in the Seychelles with her sister. There was an accident..."

"Caitlin?" he asked alarmed.

"No, fortunately not Caitlin," she said. "Hannah, her sister, was in an accident. That's why Caitlin and her mother had to go to her. Hannah's in hospital and—"

"Do you know where Caitlin's staying?" he interrupted.

"Yes, but… I'm sorry, it's not something I can share with you. I'll tell her you phoned," she added before she ended the call.

Don clenched his teeth and forced down an oath. He quickly dialed another number. Times like these, he was glad he had some influence. Finding out where Caitlin was staying in the Seychelles wouldn't be a problem. The private detective they sometimes used answered immediately.

Don was already on his way to the airport when his phone rang again fifteen minutes later. The detective had discovered where Caitlin was staying. Don swore. The place was a dump. There was no way she could stay there. Desperately, he looked around.

***

Caitlin dropped down on the bed in her hotel room. Hannah was bruised and rattled and her one arm had been broken, but she was going to be fine. From what they had been told by the police, a car had come out of nowhere as Hannah was crossing a street. At the very last minute shouts from bystanders had alerted her to the oncoming car and she'd managed to avoid a head-on hit, but she had tripped, broken her left arm, and was badly bruised.

Her face had not been injured, but her left leg and side looked very painful. Fortunately, the photo shoot she'd been here for had finished earlier in the day, so as soon as she was released from hospital, they could return home.

Caitlin frowned. There was something her sister was not telling her and tomorrow she'd make a plan to be alone with her. It was probably something she didn't want their mother to know. At least she and her mother had seen Hannah and knew she was going to be all right.

She looked around her and groaned. What a crummy place. She was exhausted. The last couple of days had been a blur. Ever since Hannah's phone call, her life had been turned upside down. She knew her mother would insist on going to Hannah as soon as she heard about the accident. Zoe had left for London to see a client, so Caitlin gladly accepted that she would have to accompany her. Even though their mother was a young sixty, it was clear that the news about Hannah's accident had upset her to an extent she was unable to function properly.

Fortunately, their passports had been in order and no visas were required for visiting the Seychelles. But she had to organize another physiotherapist to take over her patients for a week, book the tickets, find accommodation, find a shuttle to the airport, help her mother to stay calm, all while she tried not to think about the photo in which a bloody beauty queen, or whoever she was, was hanging on to Don Cavallo's arm.

She was going to forget she'd ever laid eyes on him. She'd hoped that all the nasty things she'd said in her blog would help her get over him, but this time, it didn't. She never got around to deleting the entry, so her ranting was out there in the virtual world for all to read. But he was still very much on her mind. Why was she wasting time on someone who had clearly forgotten all about her?

She got up from the bed. Enough. She was not going to think about him for the rest of the evening. Surely that would be possible?

First thing tomorrow she was going to find another place for her and her mother to stay. Her mother hadn't said anything but it hadn't been difficult to read the expression on her face when they had walked into the hotel.

All she knew when she had made the booking was that Hannah was in the Seychelles Hospital in Victoria, the main city of the island of Mahé, the biggest of the Seychelles Islands. So she looked for a place close to the hospital and on the cheaper side. There wasn't really time to look at ratings, she'd relied solely on the pictures on the website. But this place was nothing like the photos posted on the internet. "Dump" would be too kind a way to describe it. The walls were not very clean, the curtains torn, and the bedding… Shuddering, she crossed her arms.

In normal circumstances she would have asked Hannah before she booked a room, but everything had been done in such haste.

Grimacing, she looked at her suitcase, still unopened. She desperately needed a shower, but the bathroom was even tackier than the sleeping area.

There was a knock on her door. "Caitlin?" She heard her mother's voice.

Worried, she quickly moved to the door. For the first time since their arrival, she thought of her phone. It was still in her bag and switched off. Would her mother have tried to phone her? She opened the door.

But her mother was smiling. "My dear, such good news," she began, as Caitlin noticed her mum's luggage was collected behind her. A dark-haired man moved closer. For a second Caitlin's heart lurched, but it settled back down again. The man wasn't Don.

He smiled and put out his hand. "I'm Dale Cavallo, Don's brother. We met during the Wines to Whales race. Don't know if you remember me?"

Caitlin tried to smile. "Yes, I do. But what are you doing here? And Mum, why…?"

Dale motioned to another man behind him who walked into the room and picked up Caitlin's suitcase.

Dumbfounded, Caitlin tried to make sense of what was happening.

Dale cleared his throat. "Hannah had been staying in one of our hotels before the accident. There is a whole suite booked in her name with more than enough space for all of you. You can't stay here," he said and looked around, disgust obvious in his voice.

"We saw Hannah earlier today, she didn't say anything…"

"She didn't realize that a room had been booked for

another few days, but I've eased her mind about it. The duration of her stay, and yours are, of course, on the house."

"Oh, but that's not necessary, we are—"

"We insist," Dale interrupted with a smile.

For a moment, Caitlin wanted to refuse but then she looked at her mother. The expectant look she saw on her face decided for her. She couldn't refuse Dale's offer just because his brother was an idiot.

And then relief made her want to cry. It was wonderful to be able to lean on someone else for a little while. Her shoulders had been stiff with tension and she could actually feel her muscles relaxing.

"Thanks," she said, and tried to swallow the ache in her throat. "You're very kind."

Another man picked up her mother's suitcase and with a nod, both men left the room.

Dale chuckled. "Both Darryn and Don have been driving me crazy with their frantic phone calls. I was told in no uncertain terms to make sure you are taken to our hotel. Tonight."

"Darryn? Is he one of your other brothers? Does he also know Caitlin?" asked her mother as they fell in behind Dale, walking down the narrow corridor.

"He's met Caitlin but I think his main concern at the moment is Hannah," Dale said as they finally stepped out of the dingy hotel.

For the first time in three days, her mother smiled. "Oh really?" was all she said. "Does Don also know Hannah?" she asked, winking at Caitlin.

A chauffeur-driven car stopped in front of them and Dale opened the door for her mother. "As far as I know they've met, but he was very worried about you and Caitlin." He smiled.

Caitlin got into the car. Nothing Dale had said made sense. Darryn worried about Hannah. From what she recalled, they didn't like each other much. And how did

Don know she and her mother were here? Why would Don be worried about them when he was clearly involved with someone else?

She closed her eyes. Too many questions for this time of night. A bed. A clean one. That was all she wanted now. Trying to figure out what was going on would have to wait for the new day. But something warm had nestled close to her heart. She was too tired to wonder what it could be but she liked the feeling.

***

The minute his plane touched down at the airport on Mahé, Don phoned Dale.

He didn't even wait for Dale to answer. "Did you get a hold of them?" he barked.

"Hi, Don, I'm fine, thank you. How are you?" his brother said sarcastically but already the tightening around Don's chest was loosening. Dale wouldn't have joked if he'd had a problem.

"Did you put them in the hotel here in Victoria?" Don asked.

"Yes, that's where Hannah has been staying. I've moved them to one of the suites as you requested. They're probably fast asleep by now. There should be someone at the airport to pick you up."

"Thank you," Don said. "And I'm sorry—"

"That you were rude and a pain in the butt?"

"Yeah, that." Don grinned, feeling better by the minute despite the fact he hadn't been able to sleep for the past forty-eight hours.

"I can't wait to hear the real reason you and Darryn went berserk over two women."

"Darryn? What did he want?" asked Don as he walked toward the exit of the airport building. He only had an overnight bag with him, and fortunately, he had clothes in all their hotels. They often had to travel with very little notice.

"He phoned me on Monday evening, completely frantic. Probably right after you'd spoken to him."

Don frowned. "I spoke to him earlier in the day before I knew about the accident so I couldn't have said anything about it. Why did he phone?"

"He was in a state over Hannah, Caitlin's sister."

"Really? I thought he couldn't stand the sight of her," Don said as he walked out of the building. Relieved, he saw the hotel's car parked right in front of the building.

"Then you know more than I do. He's on his way. We can both ask him how he knew about the accident and why he's so upset about a woman I've never even heard of before."

"I'm getting into the car," Don said, trying to change the subject because he knew what was coming.

"And, I'm waiting to hear why you've been so upset. I thought you'd only met Caitlin that one time. Seems I have a lot to catch up on," Dale said teasingly.

As they sped through the quiet streets of Victoria, Don wondered about the same thing. Why was he so upset about Caitlin? But the thought of her distraught and alone in a dingy hotel had made him frantic. This overwhelming urge to be with her, to help her, to comfort her was such an alien feeling he wasn't sure what to make of it.

All he knew was that he had to see her as soon as possible. He put his head back against the car seat and closed his eyes. He couldn't remember the last time he'd slept properly.

CHAPTER 8

Don's warm hand cupped her cheek and she turned her face into his palm. The woodsy scent of his aftershave surrounded her and she felt safe. He murmured her name and kissed her. Lightly, like the touch of a butterfly. But she wanted more and drew his head down.

This time there was nothing light about his kiss. She was instantly transported to a place where nothing else mattered but the warmth spreading through her body and the excitement slowly building up inside her. His lips were warm, inviting, demanding, and she was unable to do anything but give him what he was asking.

Her body was going up in flames. It was hot, so hot.

Caitlin shot up in bed and switched on the bedside lamp. She gulped in air in an effort to stabilize her erratic breathing. She had to have been dreaming, but it had been so real. It was as if Don had really been here, in her hotel room. His scent still seemed to be all around her.

She leaned back against the pillows and closed her eyes. The strange events of the last few days were probably catching up with her. That was the only reason for this vivid dream. She rubbed her hand over her face and froze. His scent was on her hand. She sniffed her hand again.

Had he been here, next to her bed, kissing her? Or was she losing her mind?

Caitlin sighed and turned on her side with a grunt. She was overtired. She could not be dreaming about Don Cavallo.

***

Don was pacing the foyer when he finally saw her. It was nearly nine a.m. now and he'd been waiting to see her all this time.

Caitlin and her mother were stepping out of the lift and his heart tripped. He moved toward them. She glanced up and saw him. Her eyes narrowed, her lips tightened.

What the hell? Last night he had to use all his willpower to walk away from her. She'd been tired and not even awake. But now she was ignoring him.

"Don!" her mother cried out when she saw him. "My dear, we owe you and your brothers so much. Thank you for rescuing us last night and putting us up in your lovely hotel." She smiled and opened her arms to hug him. He looked at Caitlin over her mother's shoulder, but she was looking the other way.

"Caitlin," he said, forcing her to look at him.

"Don," she said and nodded in his direction. "Thank you. I'm sorry for the inconvenience, I'm sure other…people needed you."

Don suppressed the urge to shake her, but before he could say anything else, he heard Dale behind them.

"Good morning, everyone. I trust you slept well?" Dale asked.

"Yes, thank you. We have such a lovely suite." Caitlin's mother smiled.

"Thank you, Dale, for all your help last night." Caitlin smiled and stepped closer to Dale.

The next minute she was hugging his brother right in front of his eyes.

Swallowing a swear word, Don put his hand on Dale's shoulder and moved him away from Caitlin. "Why don't you take Mrs. Sutherland to breakfast? I want to show Caitlin something," Don said, trying to arrange a calm smile on his face.

Caitlin's mother tucked her hand through Dale's arm. "Please call me Brenda. Mrs. Sutherland is so formal. I'd love some breakfast! I can't remember the last time we ate anything…" They walked toward the dining room.

Don waited until they were through the doors before he turned back to Caitlin. "So my brother gets a hug but not me?" he asked and took her hand. "Come with me," he growled and quickly walked them toward his office just down the corridor.

She tried to pull her hand out of his, but he held on tightly.

He opened the door and motioned her inside.

"Don, really, I don't have time for this. My sister—"

"—is in the hospital and I'll take you and your mother to her in a moment."

Caitlin sighed and folded her arms. "Look, Don, you are obviously involved with someone. I don't understand what you want from me."

He put his hands in the pockets of his trousers. It was either in there or around her neck. "Oh, I'm involved with someone. Really?"

"I saw the picture," she said.

He walked toward his desk and lifted a newspaper page from the desk. "This one?" he asked and held the page out to her. She looked at it and nodded.

"I came to your room last night. I was worried sick and had to see for myself that you were fine. You nearly dragged me into the bed with you. I had to force myself to leave you and this morning…" His voice had steadily risen and he stopped talking.

Her eyes widened. "So I didn't dream it?" she whispered. "You were really there? In my room?"

He nodded. "I was in your room. I had to see you and if you hadn't been through such an ordeal, I would have woken up beside you this morning." He walked until he stood toe to toe with her. "I'm not involved with her," he said, jabbing a finger toward the picture.

"But…" Caitlin began but he shook his head and placed his hands on her shoulders.

"I know many people, men and women. But I don't cheat and I don't lie. I also don't explain myself. You either believe me or you don't."

Caitlin stared up at him, hundreds of thoughts racing through her head. She didn't even trust her own father and this man, someone she barely knew, was asking her to trust him.

The picture of him with another woman in the paper had left her bewildered and hurt. And now, if she understood him correctly, even though he wasn't going to explain the why and the how about the other woman, he thought she should trust him.

She lifted her chin and crossed her arms in front of her. What she wanted to do was burst into tears and rant and rave about everything, but not in front of Don. She could at least try to keep herself together and not fall completely apart.

Her sister was her main priority at the moment. "You're right. You don't owe me any explanations," she said coolly and walked to the door. "I'm here for Hannah and I can't think about anything else right now."

He stared at her for a moment longer then he nodded. "Fine. Let's forget you nearly pulled me into bed with you last night. Let's have breakfast, then I'll take you and your mother to your sister." The sarcasm in his words wasn't hard to catch.

He moved toward the door to open it but she quickly opened it herself and walked on to the breakfast room. She didn't need anyone to do things for her; she could open a bloody door by herself. And she hadn't pulled him into

"How is Hannah?" Don asked when he picked them up. He helped her mother into the front seat and Caitlin quickly opened the back door. But before she could get in, he was there, holding the door for her.

"Hannah seems to be fine: she's fighting with everyone." Caitlin's mother smiled. "I'm not sure about your brother, though. The last time we saw him he was storming down the hospital corridor, just about spitting fire."

"What is it with those two?" Don murmured as they drove down the street.

"Hannah is also very upset, Mum," Caitlin reminded her.

"She's just angry because she wanted to leave the hospital today and the doctor and your brother ganged up against her." Her mother smiled at Don.

"But she can go home tomorrow and wants to go directly to the airport. I'll have to see how quickly we can book seats," Caitlin said.

"Let me see if I can help," Don said, taking out his cell phone.

"It's not necessary—" Caitlin began but her mother put her hand on Don's arm.

"Thank you, Don. You and your brothers have been very kind. I hope you will let us repay you when you visit Hermanus again."

"No repayment necessary, but I would like to visit you when I'm there again," he said before he dialed a number on his phone.

"But the payment!" Caitlin began rummaging through her bag for her credit card.

"We can sort it out later," Don said in a clipped voice and ignored her hand with the card in it.

Irritated, Caitlin sat back. She could throttle the man. Why was he doing this? He started speaking over the phone. His words were precise, and minutes after her mother had given him their identity numbers, he'd given someone the instruction to book their tickets.

Caitlin put her head back against the car seat and closed her eyes. She tried to stay angry with him but whether she wanted to acknowledge it or not, it was wonderful to be taken care of. It really wasn't a big deal to organize plane tickets but feeling as emotional as she did after the last few days, everything seemed like a huge effort.

And Don and his brothers had been very kind. Why they were going out of their way to help the Sutherland women, she had no idea, but right now she didn't want to think about it. Her head was hurting and the pain just below her heart wouldn't budge.

***

As soon as he'd stopped the car in front of the hotel, Caitlin jumped out with a mumbled apology and disappeared through the swinging doors.

Her mother turned to him and put a hand on his arm. "Thank you, my dear. You and your brothers have been so kind."

He dragged his gaze back to Caitlin's mother. "It's a pleasure," he said and opened his door.

Caitlin's mother hesitated for a minute, her smile gone for the first time since he'd met her. "My husband left me and the girls when they were still very small. They find it difficult to trust anyone."

Then the smile was back, her eyes twinkling as they normally did. "The man who falls in love with any of them will have the difficult task of earning their trust. So he will have to make sure he knows exactly what his feelings are."

Don stared at her for a moment, his head reeling. Who the hell was talking about falling in love? Yeah, he wanted Caitlin. She was sexy as hell and he was a normal red-blooded male. But that was it. It wasn't as if he wanted to marry her.

The word "marry" exploded in his brain and he quickly got out of the car. This was the second time this woman had his brain working along these lines. The previous time he'd been thinking about white picket fences and Labrador dogs.

He tried to inhale some air into his lungs, but it was as if there wasn't enough oxygen around him. Caitlin's mother was standing on the other side of the car, her eyes laughing at him.

"You're a nice man, Don Cavallo. I hope I get the chance to tell your mother that," she said before she also disappeared through the swinging doors of the hotel.

One of the hotel drivers came closer. Don handed him the car keys and stood looking after him for a long time. Images of Caitlin kept playing over and over in his mind. His blood heated. With an oath, he turned around and walked into the hotel.

He had wanted a nice time with a pretty girl. That was it. He wasn't interested in anything long-term and certainly didn't have time for someone who had trust issues. This was getting too complicated. No way in hell was he going to explain his every move.

She was flying back to South Africa the next day and he was going to spend at least another two weeks here. By that time, he'd have met another pretty girl and would have forgotten all about the brown-haired, blue-eyed physiotherapist with baggage.

Besides, if he and his brothers wanted to do the Cape Epic Cycling race in March, they would have to get serious about their training. There wasn't time for women. Any women.

He stopped when a thought struck him. She couldn't even cook. Isn't that what her own mother had told him? Well, loving food the way he did, he couldn't waste time with someone who couldn't cook. Well, that clinched it. She was history.

As he walked toward his office, he grimaced. Maybe if

he told himself that a few hundred times, he might start to believe it.

CHAPTER 9

Darryn was waiting for them as Caitlin and her mother left the hotel. The receptionist had phoned them the previous evening with details of their flight. They were departing that morning and transport to the airport had been arranged.

When Caitlin had asked about the payment for the plane tickets, she was told that it had been taken care of. The same message was waiting for them when they wanted to pay for their accommodation.

Dale did say that their stay would be on the house, but she had hoped they would be able to pay without the brothers knowing about it. But the message was clear. She was still fuming and was going to tackle Don the minute she saw him. But now he wasn't here, only his brother.

"Good morning, Darryn!" her mother called out. "I thought Don…" she began as Darryn opened the door for her.

"He's picking up Hannah," he said tersely. "She…we thought it best. They'll meet us at the airport. This way, we'll waste less time."

When Caitlin got into the car, her mother looked around, her eyes huge and twinkling.

"Mum, behave yourself," she whispered.

"He has a thing for our Hannah, I'm telling you," her mother managed to whisper just before Darryn got into the car.

He was silent all the way to the airport but her mother chattered nonstop, for which Caitlin was grateful for once. The headache of the previous evening hadn't quite gone and the sleepless night she'd had wasn't helping. She had been ready for a fight with Don and now he wasn't even here and she probably wouldn't see him again.

She'd find a way to repay him for the tickets, that she promised herself. There was no way she was going to accept any more of his charity.

"...don't you agree, Caitlin?" her mother's voice penetrated her thoughts.

"Umm...sorry, Mum, I wasn't listening," she said.

"I was saying the color of the sea around these islands is something else, don't you agree?"

Caitlin stared out of the window. "Yes, it's breathtaking," she said softly, drinking in the sight.

"Next time, we'll stay longer so that we can see more of the islands," her mother continued. "Do you have any other hotels around here?" her mother asked.

"Yes, we have another one on Praslin, the other big island, but..."

Caitlin tuned out his voice and stared at the scenery along the way without registering what she was looking at. Within a few hours she would leave this island and probably never see Don again. She'd been so angry with him but now that she was leaving, there was just a big hole inside of her, the irritation and anger of only minutes before completely gone. This was what he did to her.

Normally, she was a fairly happy person who didn't get angry easily. But ever since she'd met Don, her emotions had gone haywire. One minute she was in the throes of ecstasy and the next she wanted to throw something at him.

She should just forget about him. She closed her eyes. But how she was ever going to forget the way he made her feel with just a kiss, she didn't know.

***

Don pulled up in front of the airport building. Hannah was still pale but the determined thrust of her chin had warned him not to say anything. He liked her. She spoke intelligently and yes, like her sister, had opinions about everything, but she was no airhead. Why Darryn got so annoyed with her, he had no idea.

He got out of the car just as Darryn's car pulled up behind him. The back door opened and a pair of killer legs swung out. His heart skipped a beat and he purposefully looked away. Just one person had legs like that. Damn it, he had hoped that he'd be gone before Darryn arrived with Caitlin and her mother.

"Don!" Brenda exclaimed and rushed over to him. The next minute her arms were around his neck and she was hugging him. "I'm so glad to see you," she said, laughing. "I'd been so worried that we wouldn't see you again."

She looked around as Darryn came closer. "We want to thank you again for all of your help and hospitality. And please let me know next time you're in Hermanus, I'd like to invite you over," she announced, then kissed both men.

A porter had loaded their luggage on to a trolley. Caitlin and Hannah stood next to it, both of them looking anywhere but at Don and his brother. Their mother motioned them over.

"Come on, girls, say goodbye to these nice young men. They have been so kind."

Darryn nodded in Caitlin's direction and walked over to Hannah. Caitlin walked closer to Don, her reluctance obvious.

"Goodbye, Don," Caitlin said and held out her hand. Nervously, she looked up at him. She'd hoped she and her mother would be in the airport building before Don arrived with Hannah. And now he was here, his big body right in front of her.

"Damn, Caitlin, you're killing me," he whispered and pulling her closer, he kissed her. There was just time to notice the storm in his eyes before his lips closed over hers. And then her ability to think, to rationalize, to consider, simply failed to work. His lips were warm and urgent, his tongue demanding access, which she was unable to deny him.

She forgot about her mother, the other people, where they were. Her senses went into overdrive and hitherto-unknown sensations and feelings ripped through her body. Then he lifted his head and stepped away.

"Have a nice flight," he growled before he turned back to his car.

Stunned, she turned around. Her mother was watching her with twinkling eyes and Hannah was struggling with her one arm to get the trolley going. A porter appeared, taking the trolley from her.

Caitlin tried to get the message from her brain to her legs to move, but somehow they weren't listening.

Darryn called Hannah's name and, cussing under his breath, followed her into the building. Only then was Caitlin able to move. Her mother took her arm.

"Well, I'm glad to see you're not completely stupid." Her mother grinned. "Come on, sweetheart, we have a plane to catch. Where is Hannah...? Oh, my!" her mother breathed and Caitlin stopped in her tracks.

Dumbfounded, she and her mother stared at the scene in front of them. Darryn had bent Hannah over his arm and was kissing her. Passionately. And he was taking his time about it.

Then, as if nothing had happened, he lifted his head, he caressed her hair and with a nod in their direction, left the building.

Caitlin blinked. What the hell? Had the Cavallo brothers cast a spell over them?

Hannah licked her lips and stared at them with glazed eyes. Then she shook her head and followed a grinning porter. It was obvious he'd also witnessed the kiss.

Silently, Caitlin and her mother fell in beside Hannah and they walked toward the check-in counter.

"What happened back there?" their mother asked Hannah when they reached the queue.

"Don't ask," Hannah muttered. "Please."

"Well, I, for one, can't wait to get home. My fingers are literally itching to write. Finally, my daughters are giving me some material for new stories," their mother teased.

Caitlin tried to think of something to say, but she was unable to string together a sentence, let alone a coherent objection.

***

It was only when they were waiting for their luggage in Cape Town airport that Caitlin thought about the problem of how they were going to get home. She groaned out loud.

Her mother looked at her questioningly. "What now, dear? Although I'm glad to hear you can make a sound. The two of you haven't spoken a word since we left Mahé."

"With all the rush, I hadn't thought to organize someone to pick us up. I didn't think we'd be coming back before the weekend and then Dana would have picked us up. I'm sorry, it just completely slipped my mind."

"Don't worry about it. The simplest would be to get a car. Then you can drop me off and drop the car off in Hermanus," Hannah said, leaning on the trolley. She was very pale again. She'd slept during most of the six-hour flight, but she must be exhausted and in pain.

Caitlin nodded and grabbed their suitcases from the carousel.

"We'll get a car, but you are not going to your flat," their mother said adamantly. "Look at you. You should still be in hospital," she scolded as they walked along the long corridor toward the arrivals lounge.

When they passed the doors, Caitlin looked around for a place where her mother and Hannah could wait for her while she got a car. She really hoped it wouldn't take too long. She was worried about her sister.

"That's me, isn't it?" her mother exclaimed and Caitlin looked up.

Her mother was pointing toward a uniformed man who was standing at the entrance, holding a board with the name "Mrs. Sutherland" in big, bold letters.

Her mother rushed forward and started talking to the man. Even before he nodded his head, Caitlin knew. One of the Cavallos had organized this. She wanted to be irritated, wanted to be angry, but she was just too grateful at the moment that Hannah wouldn't have to wait around any longer.

At this point, her sister was deathly white and clutching her arm. She was obviously still in pain. Hannah was also furtively looking around as if she were scared. There had to be more to Hannah's hit-and-run accident than what she was telling them and as soon as she was feeling better, she would ask her again.

The uniformed man quickly took charge and within minutes they were on the highway traveling toward Hermanus.

Her phone rang. It was a strangely long number but she answered without really thinking about it.

"Hi, this is Caitlin Sullivan."

"You okay?" Don's voice was crisp and clear. Her heart skipped a beat before bouncing around cheerfully.

"Yes, we're fine. And thank you for the car—"

"Just taking care of our customers," he interrupted.

"Please let me know when you're at home."

She could hear voices in the background.

"Just a moment," Don said then. "Darryn also wants a word."

"How's Hannah?" Darryn asked without greeting.

Caitlin looked at Hannah. Her eyes were closed and she seemed to be sleeping.

"She's okay, I think. Still pale and I think her arm hurts—"

Darryn swore loud and clear. "What is it with your sister? She should still be in hospital…" His voice faded.

"Don't mind my brother," Don said. He'd obviously taken the phone again. "He's in a filthy mood."

"Don't worry about it. About the cost for the plane tickets, the accommodation…"

"I told you, it's been taken care of. Relax and let me know when you're home," he said and then there was silence.

She slowly put her phone in her bag.

"Was that Don?" her mother asked.

"Yes. He…actually Darryn wanted to know if Hannah was okay," she quickly said to try and get her mother's attention away from herself.

Hannah opened one eye and frowned. "What is it with that guy?" she asked, irritated.

Caitlin also leaned her head back and closed her eyes. "That's what he wanted to know," she murmured with a smile.

"I'm too tired to get worked up now," Hannah said softly. "But I'll sort him out once I feel better."

Caitlin smiled with her eyes closed. "Me too." They all knew she and Hannah were talking about two different men.

CHAPTER 10

"So which one of you is going to go first?" Dale asked as soon as they sat down to dinner.

Darryn poured wine into his glass and ignored Dale.

"Don?" Dale asked.

"I don't know what you're talking about…" he began, but Dale swore and slapped his hand on the table.

"Don't give me that BS. You know exactly what I'm talking about. You and Darryn here had me jumping through all sorts of hoops to make sure the Sutherlands were fine. So don't tell me you don't know what I'm talking about. You two have a thing for the two sisters?"

Darryn took a sip of his wine. "Define thing," he said.

Dale barked out a laugh. "When two successful businessmen go insane over two women, fly in from all over the globe to make sure they are fine, forget that we are running other hotels as well, cancel meetings, putting said women up in the penthouse suite, I'd say we have a 'thing' here."

"Just being nice," said Darryn, glancing through menu.

"Nice. Is that what you call your crazy behavior of the last few days? By the way, how did you hear about

Hannah's accident?"

Darryn shrugged. "A friend."

Dale looked at Don. "Are you also only being nice?" he asked.

Don smiled and shrugged his shoulders. "We're nice guys, what can I say?" He lifted his glass.

Dale stared at them for a few moments and then he smiled. "Now I get it. You are in love with these beauties." He laughed out loud. "Wait 'til I tell Mum," he said, and rubbed his hands together gleefully.

Darryn glared at him. "Dude, mind your own bloody business."

Dale took a sip of his wine. "See? That's what I'm talking about. You are all worked up about a woman. What about you?"

Don shrugged. "Nothing to report. I met Caitlin, we went to dinner once," he said, holding up a finger. "I heard she had a problem, I helped. That's all there is to it."

Dale put his glass down slowly. "So let me get this straight. You guys," he said and pointed toward Don and Darryn, "are sure you're not in love with these two girls?"

Don choked on his wine. "No!" He saw people looking in their direction and lowered his voice. "Who the hell said anything about love?" he asked, irritated with the whole conversation.

"Since when do you get to interrogate us about women?" asked Darryn, clearly annoyed.

"Since I want to make sure the playing field is clear."

Something cold clutched Don's heart and he put his glass down slowly. "What are you talking about?"

"What playing field?" Darryn asked, his voice frosty as well.

Dale looked Don straight in the eye. "I'll start with Caitlin. I think she's gorgeous. Add to that the fact that she's sexy as hell, that she obviously cares for other people and I'm thinking…"

"Don't," Don said through clenched teeth.

"…if you're not interested, I'm going to…"

Before Don was aware of what he was doing, he was up and had a hand pressing down hard on Dale's shoulder. "I said *don't*," he snarled and walked away quickly.

Dale's laughter followed him all the way to his office.

***

Caitlin had just nodded off when the buzz of her phone woke her up. Half asleep, she answered.

"You didn't call me," Don growled in her ear.

"Don?" she asked, her voice husky from sleep.

"I asked you to phone me when you got home, and you didn't."

Rubbing her eyes, Caitlin switched on the bed light and leaned back against the pillows. She was still not quite awake. Her head felt woozy, she was tired, irritated with herself for struggling to forget about this man, and now he'd phoned again. "Don, I'm in bed, I've just fallen asleep, seriously—"

"What are you wearing?" he asked, his voice now gruff.

She looked down at herself and couldn't prevent the giggle. "A very old, very faded oversized T-shirt, nothing to have a sexy phone conversation about."

"Is that what we're having? A sexy phone conversation?" he asked in a voice that sent shivers down her spine.

"Don, don't do this," she nearly pleaded.

"Is that all that you're wearing?" he continued as if she hadn't spoken.

"No…I…" She swallowed and felt the heat creep up her face. What was she doing?

"Take it off," he ordered softly.

Her breath hitched in her throat and she was unable to speak.

"Are you wearing panties?" he asked.

"Yeah," she was able to say.

"What color?"

"Pink."

"Lace?"

"Yeah."

His breath was uneven. "Take them off."

"Don, what…?"

"Take. Them. Off," he ordered huskily.

As if in a trance, she slowly pulled down her panties and threw them to the side, not bothering to look where they fell.

"Did you take them off?" he asked.

"Yes."

"Do you know what I would do if I were there?"

"What?" she whispered, the fight, the hurt, the anger of before gone. With his voice in her ear, it was so easy to imagine him next to her. Her whole body was on fire, craving Don's touch.

"Do you remember where my hands were just before my phone rang?"

He didn't have to explain what he was talking about. She vividly remembered every touch, every kiss of his urgent lips, his hands cupping her heat. Damn it, she'd been trying to forget about that ever since…

She sat up straight and pulled the blankets over her. How could she forget? Ever since she'd seen the picture of him with another woman, she'd been trying to get him out of her head.

"Is this what you do with all those women hanging on your arms? Do you call them and talk to them like this?" she asked, the anger and hurt fortunately now back.

There was silence for a minute. "I told you I don't cheat," he finally said, the huskiness now completely gone from his voice.

Good. This Don she could deal with.

"I saw the picture of you and the woman," she said.

"And I told you I'm not involved with her—"

"And you don't explain yourself. I remember.

Goodnight, Don," she said and hung up the phone without waiting for his reply.

Her whole body was tingling. She had to try and forget about this bloody man, but damn it, he could turn her on with only his voice in her ear. How was she supposed to sleep now, let alone forget about him?

***

Cussing, Don threw his cell phone on his bed. He'd only wanted to check whether she was safe and at home. But when he'd heard her sexy, sleepy voice, his hormones simply took over like they usually did when he was around Caitlin.

Hell, he was not going to explain every movement he made. He had never done that and was not about to start now. He was a grown man, used to going his own way, doing his own thing. No way was he going to start justifying his movements because a woman had trust issues.

He stopped when he realized he was pacing his bedroom floor. Her father had walked out on them and you didn't need to be a psychologist to figure out why she was distrustful.

How any man could walk away from a woman like Caitlin's mother and her three daughters was beyond him. His own dad fiercely and unapologetically loved his mother and them. And he knew that if he loved a woman, there was no way that he would ever be able to leave her. For any reason.

He swore. There it was again. The bloody L-word. Suddenly it was part of his thought process. What the hell?

At the moment, his life was perfect. He worked hard, played hard, and was not looking for anything more complicated. And trying to teach a woman to trust him was complicated. Best to stay away from her.

Pleased with his resolution, he got into bed. The

minute he closed his eyes, though, a pair of clear blue eyes laughed at him. And his body stirred. Swearing loud and long, he turned on his side and tried again to fall asleep.

Ten minutes later, still cursing, he got up and reached for his cell phone.

He didn't have to wait long.

"Caitlin," she answered, her voice sexy and warm in his ear. And just like that, he was hard as a rock.

He took a deep breath and tried to focus on what he wanted to say to her.

"The woman in the picture? She came up to me at the airport and when she greeted me, a camera flashed nearby. I met her once before at some party, I don't even remember her name. That's it."

There was silence on the other side.

He gritted his teeth. He had explained, hadn't he? If she didn't believe him, there was nothing else he could do.

"Thanks for telling me," she said after a few seconds.

He sat down on the bed, unsure of what to say next.

"Don, I'm glad you phoned again. I don't think I've thanked you enough for all you did for us, I don't know how to repay—"

"I told you it's been handled, forget about it. There was no way I'd let you stay in that hovel." He was silent for a minute. "You could have phoned me, you know that, don't you? When you heard about your sister, you should have called me."

She caught her breath. "I don't know that. We hardly know one another—"

This time he swore out loud. "You know enough about me to know…" he began but stopped short. For what he was about to say was freaking him out. He'd nearly blurted out that she should have known he'd do anything for her. Where the hell had that thought come from?

"It's late. Go to sleep. I… Goodnight," he said quickly and ended the conversation.

***

Caitlin put the phone down. After Don's earlier phone call, she'd been unable to sleep and had been writing on her blog ever since. She was hoping that putting her jumbled thoughts into actual words might clarify her own feelings, but now she was more confused than ever.

While trying to express her feelings on her blog, she again became aware of exactly how much Don and his brothers had done for them on Mahé.

And now he'd phoned again to explain about the woman in the picture. Even though he'd said that explaining was something he never did. And strangely enough, she believed what he'd told her. She shouldn't. Men were not to be trusted, she knew that. But she believed Don. Whether it was because she wanted to believe him, she wasn't sure—and it didn't matter.

So, what did that mean? Did it mean anything? What was this ache deep inside of her?

Groaning, she got up. She had to try and get some sleep. Maybe when she was not so tired, she would be able to figure out her own feelings.

***

How long he sat with the phone in his hand, he didn't know. The only thing that he was sure of was that he'd have to stay away from Caitlin. At least until he had himself under control.

CHAPTER 11

"Mum, where on earth are you taking us?" Zoe asked. "We are way up in Kloof Street, there isn't much else ahead."

Their mother just smiled. Caitlin put her head back and stared at the traffic. It was the first week of December and it seemed as if the number of cars moving into Cape Town on this late Sunday morning had doubled since she'd been here a few weeks before. It was nearly Christmas and most people were probably on their way to the Waterfront for shopping.

She'd struggled to get into the holiday spirit this year. Holidaymakers had been flooding into Hermanus over the weekend and the little town was nearly bursting at the seams. This had always been her favorite time of year but this year she felt so…unhappy. It was probably the closest word to describe the lethargic feeling that had crept up on her.

Don hadn't contacted her since their last telephone conversation. She kept telling herself that she hadn't expected him to, but every time the phone rang or there was a knock on her door, her heart skipped a beat. Because it might be him.

It made her so mad. She didn't want to be that girl who sat at home staring at the moon, longing for her man. But that was exactly what she'd been doing the last couple of months. Lovesick. The word crept into her head and she sat up straight.

She was not lovesick. To be lovesick, she would have to be in love. Oh, hell. Nobody was in love! What a crazy thought.

"I'm going to feed Caitlin," their mother said and gave her a sideways look. "You've lost such a lot of weight and you've been moping since we returned from the Seychelles in October."

"I've been busy, Mum, not moping, there's a difference," Caitlin said and looked up at Table Mountain. The sight always took her breath away. It was always there, always looking the same.

"I know you can't cook, but you love to eat. Or, you used to love to eat. Today, I'm going to make sure you enjoy a good meal and I'm going to see to it that you laugh a little. Dana is with us and we've picked up Zoe and Hannah. I haven't seen my girls for quite some time and from what I've heard, both your sisters will be away from tomorrow until Christmas. So, there's no more reason to mope."

Caitlin ignored her mother's probing look and turned around to look at her sisters. "I know Hannah is off to Paris, but where are you going?" she asked Zoe.

Zoe shrugged. "One of the Cavallo brothers contacted me, it seems—"

"Which one?" Hannah and Caitlin asked simultaneously.

"Dale, I think he said."

"Why?" Hannah wanted to know.

"They need an interior decorator for a new hotel they're building near the Kruger National Park. And apparently one of the other brothers mentioned what I do." She frowned. "I would like the job, but I didn't much like the way he talked to me, so I'll have to see."

"Mmmm, another Cavallo," Dana said while Caitlin's mother parked her car. "They seem to pop up in all your conversations. There isn't perhaps another brother?" she asked, grinning.

"There actually is," Hannah muttered. "David. He used to be a journalist before he joined his brothers in the hotel business."

"A pity," Dana grimaced and got out of the car. "I hate journalists."

"Well, girls," Caitlin's mother said, "you're in for a surprise. Come on!"

Caitlin opened the car door and looked over her shoulder. Far below them lay Cape Town and right at the bottom was the harbor.

"Well, the setting can't be better," she said and looked up to see the name of the restaurant. And did a double take. Rosa's. Wasn't this…?

She inhaled sharply and swung around. "Mother, this is Don's mother's restaurant, isn't it? What were you thinking?" she hissed but her mother hugged her quickly.

"Rosa has kindly invited us for lunch, so behave," she said and stepped into the restaurant.

Feeling numb, Caitlin looked at Hannah.

"Did you say Don's mother's restaurant?" Hannah asked, a stunned expression on her face.

Caitlin nodded.

"Did you know about this?" she asked Zoe, who was just looking fed up.

"Of course not. I didn't even like the sound of this Dale guy's voice! Why on earth would I willingly spend time with his mother?"

"Well, I'm sorry for you guys, but the smells coming from this place are truly divine. I'm going in," Dana said and walked into the restaurant.

Their mother poked her head out of the door. "Come on, girls." She laughed and beckoned them closer. "You're in for a treat!"

Hannah looked as if she was going to bolt any minute. Zoe took her arm and also pulled Caitlin closer. "Let's have lunch. The sooner we start, the sooner we can get our mother away from here," Zoe grumbled.

Before they'd reached the door, a smiling, dark-haired woman appeared. It was easy to see where the Cavallo men got their looks. She was wearing a chef's top and opened her arms wide when she saw them.

"The beautiful Sutherland women and their beautiful friend. Come on, I've made my special pasta dish for you." She smiled and managed to hug them at the same time. She spoke perfect English and there was just a distant trace that it wasn't her first language.

She took Caitlin's face in her hands and stared at her for a moment.

"Beautiful," she said softly and turned to take Hannah's face in her hands. She muttered something in what sounded like Italian before moving to Zoe and peering deeply into her eyes. Dana, the odd woman out, was given a quick, charming smile that spared her the same treatment.

Rosa threw her hands up into the air. "Gorgeous. All of you." She nodded. "Now I understand." She smiled and ushered them into the restaurant before Caitlin could ask what it was she understood.

Their mother was talking to a dark-haired man outside at the back of the restaurant and Caitlin's heart skipped a beat. But when he turned around, she realized it was an older version of Don. His face was craggy, his hair showed signs of gray, but the smile was unmistakably Cavallo.

Don's mother rushed toward him. "Look at them, Michael. Beautiful, all of them," she laughed and pointed in their direction.

The man stepped closer and smiled. "They are, indeed, my love, they are indeed," he muttered, his eyes twinkling. "I'm Michael. I understand you've met my sons?" he asked

Caitlin and she nodded. The whole thing was so surreal. She wasn't dreaming, was she?

She looked at her friend and sisters. They looked as dazed as she was feeling.

"Sit down, please," Rosa said and pulled out chairs. "The boys should be here soon. I thought we'd sit outside. It is such a beautiful day and you can see the harbor from here."

"Boys?" Hannah asked quickly.

Michael smiled and helped Hannah into her chair. "She means our sons. They will always be their mama's boys, though."

Caitlin's head was reeling. If her bewildered brain understood correctly what was going on, the Cavallo brothers were also going to be here.

She glanced in Zoe and Hannah's direction. Both of them were frowning and were looking daggers at their mother.

"Isn't this nice?" her mother asked, blithely ignoring her daughters' scowls.

Michael smiled knowingly and lifted a bottle of red wine. "Rosa recommends this wine with the special dish she made for you today, but if you would prefer something else, just let me know," he said and walked around the table, pouring wine for all of them.

"To your lovely girls, Brenda." He smiled and lifted his glass.

"And to our boys," Rosa said, lifting her glass.

Michael looked at the four of them and chuckled. "It would seem these two ladies have put you in a spot," he said.

"I didn't know you'd met Don's parents," Caitlin said and looked pointedly at her mother.

"Well, the last time I came to see my publisher we had lunch here and I met the chef," she replied with a poker face.

"Yeah, right," Zoe grumbled, but smiled at their

mother. "Something smells delicious, so you're forgiven, Mum." She raised her glass.

Hannah looked at Caitlin and they both rolled their eyes. "We'll talk later," Hannah said but a smile hovered around her mouth.

"I've left my sous-chef in charge so that I can get to know you girls." Rosa smiled and sat forward on her chair. "Caitlin, you are the physiotherapist who worked on Donato's back?" she asked.

"Donato?" Caitlin asked praying fervently that the heat she felt creeping up her neck would not be visible to anyone else. Worked on his back now sounded so...so intimate.

"She calls Don that. It was her father's name." Michael smiled and touched his wife's shoulder.

The small gesture warmed Caitlin's heart. That was what she would love to have, one day.

Rosa was still looking expectantly at her. "Yeah, I...I was on duty during a race that he, well actually, all your sons took part in. And then I treated him in my rooms in Hermanus again."

Rosa smiled and turned to Hannah.

"And you know Darryn?" Rosa asked Hannah.

"Yes, we've met," she said.

Rosa nodded her head and looked at Zoe.

"And you will be working with our Dale, I believe?" she asked Zoe.

"I don't know. We'll have to see." Zoe smiled.

"And you, Dana, must meet our David." She laughed and sat back, looking very pleased with herself.

Caitlin caught a movement on her left and turned her head. And there they were. The Cavallo brothers. Her eyes met Don's. Her heart simply leapt up.

"You're here!" their mother called out and stood up. She hesitated. "Any problems?" she asked, frowning.

"Relax, Mum. Fortunately, the press don't know we're all back in Cape Town." David smiled.

Rosa relaxed and returned his grin. "Good. Keep it that way. Come and sit, I've cooked your favorite."

David smiled and stepped closer. "Mum, where did you get these beauties?" His gaze landed on Caitlin and he walked around the table to her side. "I know this one," he said, then bent down to kiss her soundly.

***

His brain was telling him to move, to smile, to do something, but his legs just wouldn't listen. Don could only stare. At Caitlin. At her face, her hair, her mouth, the soft curve of her chin. And he could drown in the blue of her eyes. She'd lost weight.

Breathe. He wasn't breathing. He should breathe.

He'd arrived in Cape Town the previous day and couldn't ignore his mother's invitation to come to lunch. He'd missed his parents. To see Caitlin sitting here, in this restaurant that was so much a part of him, was so unreal—and the last thing he had expected.

He saw Dave bend down to kiss Caitlin and his body moved forward. Quickly. Unceremoniously, he shoved his brother aside and sat down next to Caitlin.

"Hi," he said, and she smiled. And all the resolutions of the last couple of months now sounded so silly. Because now she was here, in his mother's restaurant, he couldn't for the life of him remember why he should stay away from her. He took her hand and put it on his leg. And kept it there. Only then was he able to breathe and look around him at the others.

***

The lunch plates had been removed ages ago, but their little group still lingered over coffee. The sun had disappeared behind the mountain and a lovely, cool breeze was coming in from the sea. Caitlin lifted her face up.

Everything was perfect. Her mother, best friend, and sisters were with her and a gorgeous man kept looking at her. What more could a girl want?

The hollow, empty feeling of the last few weeks had disappeared somewhere between Rosa's amazing pasta dish and the blackberry-flavored Shiraz Michael had served them. Don's leg rubbing against hers probably had something to do with it too.

For the first time in a long time, she felt content. She was so aware of Don right beside her. He kept touching her and she was struggling to follow what the others were talking about. She tried to focus and gathered that the conversation had moved to the brothers' cycling.

"Have you ever thought of cycling professionally?" asked Dana, looking at the men.

Dale shrugged. "We all belong to the same club where some of the guys race professionally. But our business keeps us too busy. Besides, cycling is just to keep us out of trouble. At least, that's what our mum says." Dale bent over to kiss his mother.

"Does anyone there use stimulants?" asked Hannah. "I've seen a series on Netflix and it's apparently quite common among cyclists."

"No, not all cyclists use performance-enhancing drugs," Darryn said gruffly, frowning at Hannah.

"The whole thing has given cycling a bad name. Riders were accused of doing transfusions of additional red blood cells so they'd have more energy. It became popular about a decade ago when tests were developed that detected other drugs. But, hopefully the spotlight that was put on all the doping programs will prevent others from trying to do the same," said Don.

While he was talking, she had a reason to just look at him. He talked calmly with authority and listened whenever one of his brothers made a comment. He caught her eye and abruptly stopped speaking.

"Don, you were saying?" his dad asked.

Don gave him a blank look before he continued talking. When someone else started speaking, he bent his head.

"When you look at me like that I can't concentrate," he whispered, his soft breath tickling her neck.

A deliciously warm feeling opened up inside her and she smiled at him over her shoulder.

His eyes darkened and he grabbed her hand again.

"…Cape Epic race," Darryn was saying.

"Sounds…epic." Zoe smiled.

"That it is," Michael said.

Rosa put her hands over her ears. "I don't want to hear about it. It's dangerous."

"Mum, it's not that bad," Darryn began but she gave him a withering look.

"Not that bad? Ten days and twenty thousand kilometers. You're all crazy!" she exclaimed.

David put his arm around her shoulders. "Mum, you're exaggerating as always. Eight days and eight hundred kilometers. And we're breathing in fresh air and enjoying nature while doing it."

"One or all of you could get hurt. Didn't one guy break his collarbone last year?"

David put a hand on his mother's arm. "Cracked it, Mum. There's a difference."

Rosa pointed in the direction of Caitlin, her sisters, and Dana. "Why don't you marry one of these lovely girls and make babies? Then you'll stop putting your lives in danger. I would like some grandchildren before I die."

She jumped up and pulled at Caitlin's mother's hand. "Come on, Brenda, I want to show you something in the kitchen."

Caitlin's breath had hitched in her throat when Rosa uttered the words "marry" and "babies." A clear picture of a dark-haired baby boy momentarily flashed before her eyes. She blinked and looked around her. Everyone was staring after Rosa and for the first time since they had sat down, it was quiet around the table.

Michael cleared his throat. "Where will the race be next year?" he asked into the silence.

"We don't know yet," Don said. "They only release that information later."

"Have you started training?" Michael asked.

"Don and Darryn have been training like madmen on Mahé," said Dale. "In between meetings, they were riding. Hard. As if they were being chased by a thousand bulls. I've never seen anything like it," he said with a straight face and just chuckled when he got a dirty look from Darryn. "I've started out slowly like those who know, recommend. I plan to increase the hours I spend on my bike while I'm in Cape Town."

"How many kilometers do you do a day?" Zoe asked.

"At this point we do about seven hours a week. That will increase up to fifteen hours just before the race," David said. "You have to enter as a two-rider team. Don and Darryn ride together and Dale and I make up a team. It's fun," he said.

"And your poor bodies?" Caitlin couldn't help saying. "Is your back okay?" she asked Don with a frown. "Should you be exercising this hard?"

"It's not the first time I'm doing this," Don said with a small smile.

"Of course, you're a physiotherapist, I'd nearly forgotten. That's great. We'll be needing the help of one, Caitlin," David said and leaned forward in his chair. "Especially closer to the race. We'll be helping Don this weekend in Hermanus. Any chance of a session with you on Friday?"

"Get your own physio," Don growled but Caitlin ignored him.

"Of course, I'll help you." She bent down and picked up her bag. "Let me give you my contact details," she said and fished out a business card. Before she could hand it over to David, however, Don grabbed it and tucked it into his shirt pocket.

David just laughed. "I'll call you," he said at the same time her mother and Rosa returned and everyone got up.

"We have to go, Rosa. All your other diners have left," her mother said before hugging the other woman. "This has been so special."

Caitlin stood up reluctantly. This day should not have to end. It had been one of those perfect few hours out of time.

She looked up at Don. "Bye," she said.

"I'll walk you to the car," he said and took her hand.

Just before she climbed in, he came closer. "I'll phone you tonight. I'd like to take you out again."

Her legs wobbled and she grabbed hold of the car door. "Okay," was all she was able to say before Zoe shoved her inside.

"You should write about these guys on your blog," Dana said loud enough for everyone to hear before she got into the car.

"What blog?" Darryn asked.

Caitlin pulled a face at Dana. The last thing she wanted to mention was her blog. Her last entry didn't paint a very flattering picture of Don. Although she hadn't mentioned any names, he would know immediately she'd been describing him when he read it.

She glanced out of the window, but Don was speaking to his dad. Hopefully, he'd missed Dana's words.

Her mother pulled away amid shouts and as their car made its way down the hill, the last thing she saw was Don's hand in the air, waving goodbye.

Would he really phone her this time around? More importantly, did she want him to? For a minute, she tried to think seriously about the last question, but then sighed. She might fool other people, but she couldn't fool herself. Yes, she definitely wanted him to phone and yes, of course she wanted to go out with him again.

She glanced around again and smiled. Whether he'd

phone or not, it was a delicious feeling to see a man staring after you.

***

In silence, they all stared after the car as it disappeared down the hill.

"I hope one of you made a date with at least one of those stunning women," their dad said and slapped them all on the shoulders in turn.

"You will all die bachelors," their mother grumbled as she walked back into the restaurant. "And I will never have grandbabies!" she called out, throwing her hands in the air.

Don chuckled with his brothers, but his strange reaction to his mother's words surprised him. Usually he fled in the opposite direction when the words "marry" and "babies" popped up in conversation but, strangely enough that afternoon, when his mother had first mentioned those words, they hadn't sounded so scary.

"I have to work with Zoe, and work and pleasure don't mix," Dale said.

"Well, she's not the only one who was here. What about the tall one?" their father asked Dale. "It's easy to see why she's a model."

Dale glanced at Darryn and smiled. "You know, Dad, that's not a bad idea…" he began but Darryn grabbed him around the neck and pushed him into the restaurant. David followed them.

"And you?" his dad asked. "You like this Caitlin?"

Don just nodded.

"You couldn't keep your hands off her." His dad smiled. "First time I've seen you like that."

Don thought about it for a minute.

"Yeah?"

"Yeah." His dad nodded. "So, did you make a date?"

"Oh, yeah." Don smiled.

"That's my boy." His dad grinned before he walked

back into the restaurant.

It was a few minutes before Don realized he was standing alone on the pavement, smiling like an idiot.

CHAPTER 12

"Okay, I'm off to the airport," Hannah said and rummaged around in her bag. "Passport, visa, cards. I'm ready for Paris," she said and picked up her small suitcase. "Keep the key. I'll get it from you next weekend when I'm back."

"Thanks, Hannah." Caitlin smiled and hugged her sister. "And don't worry. I'm only going on a date with Don, that's it."

Hannah bit her lip. "I know. It's just…I don't want you to get hurt. Don looks like a nice guy, but then I used to think Darryn was a nice guy until…" She stopped speaking and shook her head.

"Until what?" Caitlin asked. "Obviously something happened between the two of you, but you've never spoken about it."

Hannah looked at her watch and opened the front door. "I promise to tell you someday. But now, I don't have time. Enjoy Cape Town." She smiled. "This is the first time you'll be staying in my flat for a date, isn't it?"

"Yes, but I'm not only here for the date. I'm hitting the shops this afternoon. Zoe is meeting me at the Waterfront. It's such a pity you can't join us," Caitlin said.

"Next time," Hannah said and then she was gone.

Caitlin closed the door and leaned against it for a moment. Trying to stay cool in front of Hannah had been exhausting. She didn't want to let on exactly how excited she really was.

When Don had whispered in her ear that he'd phone her, she'd promised herself that she was not going to sit around and wait for her phone to ring. But of course that was exactly what she'd been doing when it did ring. And all she really remembered now about the phone call was that she'd breathlessly agreed to a date with him in Cape Town.

She'd left Hermanus early that morning and sang the whole way to Cape Town. And here she was, as excited as a schoolgirl on her first date. She checked the time. There was about an hour before she'd be meeting Zoe. Running back to her room, she smiled. She knew exactly what she wanted to buy.

***

This is a sexy outfit. Caitlin turned so that she could check out the back. Zoe had seen the strapless top and she'd found the short skirt. The combination was exactly what she'd been looking for. The outfit was smart but casual and, most importantly, she felt comfortable in it.

She'd been ready an hour ago, and now she had half an hour to kill before Don picked her up, way too much time to think. Was this the right thing to do? Should she have agreed to go out with Don one more time?

Breathe in and out, in and out. Caitlin exhaled and walked through to the lounge. She'd watch television until Don arrived. It was too late to second-guess herself at this point and anyway, this time she knew what to expect. They'd have dinner, they'd chat and when he dropped her off, that would be that. She would not expect a phone call from him; he didn't do that. At least she knew that now.

Just before she sat down, the doorbell rang. Smiling

secretly, she walked to the door. It would seem she was not the only one who was early.

***

He couldn't stop looking at her. Ever since she'd opened the door for him that night, he was having trouble focusing on anything else but the way her short skirt left her long legs bare and the way the frilly top hugged her curves. As he helped her into the car, he'd caught a glimpse of sexy cleavage and he'd been just about drooling ever since.

He had to have spoken because here they were, sitting in The Test Kitchen in Woodstock, South Africa's number-one restaurant at the moment. The restaurant featured in all the food magazines and had one of the top chefs in the country, but he might as well have been eating dust.

He held her hand in his all the way from the car and now he caught a whiff of her scent every time he brought his glass to his mouth. All he tasted was her fragrance and he hardly took any notice of what he was eating.

They had finished their meal but an unknown hunger was still slicing through him like a sharp knife. And he now knew that mere food would never be able to assuage this craving. He wanted Caitlin.

Caitlin swallowed. She was trying so hard to appear cool and used to everything around her but she knew she was failing miserably. The setting of the restaurant alone took her breath away; the décor of the place was amazing, the food out of this world, and then there was her date. It was clear he was well-known in the restaurant and was treated with the utmost respect. This table had been carefully chosen, giving them privacy.

And to add to the fairytale atmosphere, Don had been making love to her all through the meal. Whether he was drinking wine or eating a morsel of food bite by bite, every movement seemed sexual, focused on her. His gaze never left hers.

They were sitting in a secluded spot and could have been alone on an island. He kept touching her in ways that made her feel like the most beautiful woman in the world. It was a heady feeling and maybe the reason she felt so lightheaded. The air around them was heavy and thick with sexual tension, making it difficult to breathe.

She tried to think of something to say. "Zoe tells me you are planning another hotel near the Kruger National Park," she began.

He nodded, picked up her hand and rubbed it against his face. She promptly forgot what she wanted to add.

"Don…" she whispered.

He dropped her hand and his disappeared under the table.

"Have I told you how sexy you look tonight?" he asked as his hand landed just above her knee.

All the sensations swirling around inside her, left her breathless. Don closed the gap between them and now their lips were centimeters apart.

"I can't do this," he said, his voice strained.

"Do…do what?" she stammered, not sure what he meant.

"Sit here and look at you when all I want is for you to be wrapped around me and for me to be buried so deep inside of you that you wouldn't be able to see straight." His eyes glowed in the dark.

Within seconds her blood heated and simmered just below the surface. Nobody had ever said that to her.

"Don," she whispered, licking her dry lips. "I…" she tried to explain how overwhelmed she felt but he bent down and kissed her.

His scent surrounded her, reeled her in and just like that, the simmering turned into a raging fire. Her clothes felt too tight, her body too small.

He lifted his head and like a drowning man, gulped in

some air. "We have got to get out of here," he growled, then hauled her up.

"Tab," he told the waiter who came toward them and then they were walking to the exit of the restaurant. Trembling, she was unable to do anything but follow him out to the street.

***

How they got to Hannah's flat was a mystery to Don. He didn't think he'd ever driven that fast. And now he was so hard, he might burst if she didn't get the bloody door unlocked within the next few seconds.

He grabbed the key from her and unlocked the door. Within seconds he had her up against the wall. While his heart was thundering, he gulped in some much-needed air. "Are you sure this is what you want?"

Her smile told him all he needed to know.

Finally, he could get his hands and mouth on her. Her eyes were wide, her lips trembling, and he dove in for a kiss. Her soft body wrapped around him and he was lost. Desire for the woman in his arms reared its head and roared through his blood. He had to have her: nothing else mattered.

He crushed her to him, their tongues met, fought, became entangled. Trying to touch her everywhere, he skimmed his palms up and down her sides. Raw need clawed its way up inside him. In an effort to gain control, he lifted his mouth from hers and buried his face in the curve of her throat.

Wave after wave of sensory impulses racked her body. Caitlin tried to savor everything that was happening to her, but the attack on her senses was relentless. Don's hands and lips were everywhere and she was burning up.

She had to touch him, had to feel him under her

fingers. As if he could read her mind he lifted his head and yanked his shirt over his head without unbuttoning it. And the six-pack that had haunted her dreams for months now was finally right in front of her and she was free to touch it. Touch him.

Her hands spread over his torso and she reveled in the feel of his smooth, hard muscles under her fingers. They were standing hip to hip, his need throbbing against her. With a groan, he bent down and caught her lips with his again.

Wrapping her arms around him, she leaned into his hard, solid body. The depth of her passion, her need, her craving for Don, staggered her. No matter how this was going to end, this was one night she was not going to forget. Ever.

He lifted his head, his eyes smoldering. His hands grazed the bottom part of her breasts. "You okay with this?" he whispered, flicking a thumb over her protruding nipples.

Incapable of speech, she nodded and without taking his eyes from hers, he gently pushed down the top she was wearing so that her breasts sprang free.

His eyes followed the movement of his hands and he stopped breathing. With a groan, he cupped her breasts and he put his forehead against hers.

"Do you mean to tell me," he growled, his hands caressing her sensitive flesh, "that you were sitting next to me tonight and you weren't wearing a bra?"

Again, she could only nod. Her knees had turned to rubber and she had to hold on to him to stay upright.

He barked out a laugh. "A bloody good thing I didn't know, otherwise I might have been arrested for what I would have done in public," he said, and glanced over his shoulder. Then he picked her up. Her legs folded around him and for one glorious moment her breasts nestled against his skin.

While he was walking in the direction of the dining

room, his lips found hers again. The kiss was hot and wet and swept her right into the middle of a brewing storm.

Her over-stimulated senses delighted in the sandalwood of his scent, the feel of his skin under her fingers, the sounds emanating from his throat, the gentle yet adamant touch of his hands, the texture of his hair.

He lowered her onto the table without taking his mouth from hers, his only focus to give as much pleasure as was humanly possible.

She lifted her head, her eyes liquid blue. With unsteady fingers he combed through her hair and she fell backward on her elbows. His heart tripped and stopped for a moment. She was exquisite. Lying there, her breasts swollen, her lips still wet from his kisses, she was irresistible.

He fitted perfectly between her legs, was his last rational thought. Like a man dying of thirst, he bent down to suckle one nipple while his hands skimmed up her long, smooth legs.

Caitlin was in a sea of sensation, her only concern that Don might stop what he was doing. Every stroke of his hand drove her further and further up a steep mountain. An ache throbbed where their bodies met. She could feel moisture gathering exactly there, where she needed him most.

His hands skimmed up her legs again, up and up until they met satin and lace. His eyes darkened when he discovered she was ready for him. Without taking his eyes off her, he slipped his fingers underneath the elastic. When skin touched skin, she couldn't prevent the moan escaping her throat.

"Bedroom?" He ground out the words without removing his hand.

She shook her head, gasping for air. "No, here," she got out, lifting her hips "I can't wait."

"I was going to go slow," he said, zipping down his pants, "but you make it impossible."

"Later," she panted. "Slow is overrated."

He barked out a laugh and brought out protection for her from his pocket before he kicked his pants away. She followed his movements. *Wow.* Involuntary, she licked her lips.

"Like what you see?" He teased before he slowly entered her.

She lifted her arms. "Oh, yeah." She smiled and gathered him close.

And then the gentle teasing was gone. In its place, an overwhelming need to become part of him filled her belly. He pushed slowly into her, his eyes never leaving hers. When she thought she couldn't possibly accommodate more of him, she discovered that her body was capable of so much more.

Don tried to reel himself in, tried to hold back so he could give her all the pleasure he was capable of giving, but when her velvety heat surrounded him, he had to let go. The pleasure was so intense, so overwhelming, it was impossible not to.

He kissed her again, his tongue urgently looking for hers while his thumb caressed the sensitive bud where all her nerve endings came together. She bucked under him and his arms brought her closer to him so that it was impossible to know where he ended and where she began.

"Don!" she cried out as her body quickly adapted to his rhythm. He tried to focus on her lovely face, but a red haze moved in front of his eyes and with a groan he surrendered to the torrent of emotion. With her name on his lips, they soared for a nanosecond before they both tumbled down and down and down to a place far below.

CHAPTER 13

Slowly, Caitlin became aware of her surroundings. She lifted her head. So they had made it to the bed eventually. She had no clear recollection of that. Don. She quickly turned her head but she was alone.

A noise from the direction of the kitchen told her he was still around. She stretched, feeling sore in unfamiliar places. Heat crept up her face and she giggled. Last night was a kaleidoscope of tangled limbs and long, wet, lingering kisses, of mingling breaths and sighs. She couldn't get enough of him and he had been as insatiable.

At times she'd been sure she'd reached the limit for bodily pleasure, only to learn time and time again that pleasure had no boundaries. Not when she was with Don.

"Coffee?" Don walked in, carrying a tray. He was wearing only his pants and at the sight of his muscled body, her mouth instantly became dry.

Caitlin moved up against the pillows, trying not to look at him. She clutched the sheet with both hands.

"Modest this morning, are we?" Don teased and sat next to her. He put the tray on a little table next to the bed and pulled the sheet down.

"Don!" she cried and tried to cover herself up again.

But he held on tightly.

"You are a beautiful, sexy woman and I've seen every centimeter of your body. Don't," he said when she tried to pull up the sheet again.

Then he simply picked her up and put her on his lap. She opened her mouth to protest, but he kissed her and she forgot what she wanted to say. Lights exploded behind her eyes and she gave herself up to the joy of his hands on her body.

When he pulled her underneath him, she held out her arms, modesty completely forgotten. This was where she wanted to be and where she would gladly spend every waking hour.

***

Don buttoned up his shirt while staring at the sea. Hannah's flat had a wonderful view over the water and one could even catch a glimpse of Robben Island on a bright day like this. He grinned and shook his head. Caitlin had ordered him out of the room. They'd been trying to get dressed for the past two hours.

But every time he'd caught just a glimpse of her breasts or her long legs, he just had to touch her again. And touching always led to more. This was a first for him. This lingering on, the morning after. In fact, staying over was a first for him. He usually left before the woman fell asleep, no sneaking out but no staying over, either. But with Caitlin, everything was just so different.

He glanced at his watch. He had another few minutes to spare before he had to leave for the airport. There was nothing he'd like more than to spend the day with Caitlin. But even though it was Sunday, his brothers were waiting for him; they had a hotel to build.

Even before she appeared in the doorway he turned around. As if he'd known she'd be there. And he stared. She was dressed casually in shorts and a T-shirt. Her long hair was loose and hanging down her back. His fingers were already itching to touch it; how the hell was he ever going to leave here today? Even before the question was completely formed in his head, he'd reached her.

There were questions in her eyes. Questions he didn't have clear answers for at that moment. Something was swirling inside of him, trying to fall into place. The feeling left him vulnerable, not a sensation he was comfortable with.

Something was different, Caitlin sensed even before Don kissed her. His eyes were bright, his stare quizzical. His hands folded over her arms, his touch a little rough as he pulled her in for a searing kiss.

She wrapped her arms around him, feeling she had to try and soothe him. When their lips touched, however, the flame that had burned so brightly the night before was instantly back and roaring in her ears.

His hands moved urgently to her shorts and he opened the button. She pushed it down while he opened his pants.

Then, without taking his lips from her, he lifted her against the wall. Clasping her legs around him, she poured everything he made her feel into the kiss. He cupped her bottom while the fingers of his other hand explored her soft folds.

She lifted her head to try and get oxygen into her lungs.

"Look at me," he demanded and pushed into her.

He began to move and she tried to hold his gaze, tried to focus on his face, but with the second thrust, she spun out of control. He called her name and she got lost in a sea of sensation.

It was the most beautiful thing he'd ever seen. Caitlin's head was thrown back, her arms were twined around his neck, and her lips curved upward in a smile. She was enjoying their lovemaking; she was taking pleasure from his touch. And she wasn't ashamed to show her reaction. The thought that he was responsible for her smile was intoxicating and he gripped her ass in both his hands. He wasn't done with her yet.

She exhaled and opened her eyes. "I didn't know it was possible," she whispered.

"What?" he asked, still buried deep inside her.

"Passion," she said and moved against him. "I didn't know it could take over your body like this," she groaned. Her words touched his soul and he picked up the pace.

"There's more, baby, just hang on," he murmured, and took her with him on the wildest ride he'd ever been on.

***

"I'll call you," he said and pulled her head down through the window of his car for a last kiss.

"You don't have to promise anything," she said just before he kissed her.

He frowned, playing with her hair. "I'll call you," he repeated before he drove away. He glanced in the mirror just before he turned into the street. She was still standing where he'd left her.

Damn it, he was already so late, but he just had to go back for one more kiss. The company plane would have to wait a little longer for him. With a quick look behind him, he put the car in reverse and sped backward.

Caitlin rushed forward even before he stopped.

"What's wrong?" she asked and leaned down.

"I just had to," he pulled her head down, "kiss you again," he said, just before his lips touched hers.

This time, when he looked in his mirror, she was smiling, her fingers resting on her lips. He groaned out loud and stepped on the pedal. He had to get to the airport, otherwise he'd have a lot of explaining to do.

***

"And?" Zoe asked over the phone. "What happened?"

Caitlin looked in the rearview mirror of the car before she changed lanes. She dearly loved her sisters, but at this moment she would have preferred to be left alone to sort out her jumbled thoughts.

"He spent the night," she said, and winced when Zoe screamed loudly.

"What? What happened to 'I'm taking this slowly?'" Zoe asked, mimicking Caitlin's voice.

Caitlin sighed. How did she explain something she didn't quite understand herself? She hadn't gone on a date with Don with the idea of ending up in bed with him. But the look in his eyes when she'd opened the door, the way he'd touched her all through the evening, the way he cared about what she wanted—simply went to her head. She'd been seduced and had willingly participated. The images spinning around in her mind from the previous night still had her blushing.

"Zoe, I…" she began and then stopped. Unfamiliar feelings were flooding her entire system. She hadn't been able to put a name to them yet: she only knew she was happy. Deliriously happy. And at the same time she knew that it wouldn't last. But for now, driving back to Hermanus on this glorious December day, her body still singing after last night, she was glad to be alive.

"You like him, don't you?" Zoe filled the silence.

"Yes, I like him. But we are worlds apart. I mean, he left this morning for a meeting with his brothers about building another hotel. It's just so way out of my frame of reference, I…I don't know."

It was silent for a moment. "And? How was it?" Zoe asked.

Caitlin sighed. How do you describe the most extraordinary night of your life?

It was quiet for a moment.

"That good, hey?" Zoe asked, the smile in her voice obvious.

"Yeah. That good," Caitlin said and swallowed the lump welling up in her throat.

She heard Zoe's sigh over the line and giggled, wiping the stupid tears from her eyes.

"Do you think he'll phone?" Zoe asked.

Caitlin sniffed. This was easier to answer.

"He said he would, but I'm not holding my breath. It was a one-time thing for him, Zoe. You know what men are like."

Zoe sighed. "Unfortunately, I do. Are you going to be all right, though?" she asked.

"I'll be fine. Now, tell me about your new project," she demanded and tried to listen while Zoe launched into a detailed description of her plans for the interior of the latest block of offices she was doing.

"…and then that bloody Dale wanted me to fly up today…" Zoe's voice cut through her thoughts.

"Dale. As in Dale Cavallo?" Caitlin asked.

"Yes, Dale as in Dale Cavallo. I told you he contacted me about the hotel they plan to build next to the Kruger National Park, remember?"

"Oh, yes, I do remember. Have you agreed to do it? Last time you spoke about it, you weren't very taken with Dale."

"No, I haven't agreed to anything," Zoe said hotly. "He said he'd phone so that we could arrange a meeting where we'd discuss the whole thing properly, but I never heard from him after the lunch at his mother's restaurant. And then he had the gall to phone this morning and expect me to fly up to Johannesburg immediately."

Though she loved her sister, Caitlin tuned Zoe's voice out. She had her own problems with a Cavallo. She didn't want to hear Zoe's as well.

***

In frustration, Don threw his cell phone on the bed. What the hell does technology help if you didn't have any contact with the outside world? When Darryn had used the word *remote* to describe the guesthouse in which they'd be staying, he hadn't realized he'd meant it literally. And normally he wouldn't have minded.

But he'd told Caitlin he'd phone and wanted to keep his promise. But even more than that, he wanted—no, needed—to hear her voice. He wanted to phone her as soon as the plane had landed, but his phone had kept ringing with urgent calls. And then Darryn had been there to pick him up.

They had the meeting in Sabie where they still had cell phone and internet connection but Darryn had booked them into this guesthouse for the next couple of days because it was closest to where the hotel was to be built, so this was where he wanted to shoot the ad for the hotel. And when Don was finally alone in his room and wanted to phone Caitlin, he discovered there was no reception.

Usually, after spending a night with someone, he'd wait at least a week before he'd phone again. It was his way of making sure she'd understand not to expect anything more. Sometimes, he'd forget altogether.

But after his night with Caitlin, he wanted to speak to her, wanted to talk about last night, wanted to know if she was okay. Did she have a nice day? Did she think about him?

His eye fell on the landline phone next to his bed and he smiled. Maybe she had a landline at home. He quickly dialed the telephone service and waited and waited. After several minutes, a sleepy voice answered and he asked for her number. No, sleepy-voice said, no landline for the lady.

Don felt like throwing the phone against the wall. Damn it. But okay, calm down, he'd be able to talk to her the next day. He had the number of her rooms. Feeling more settled, he walked to the window and opened the curtains.

There were no electrical lights to compete with the stars and they shone brightly in the sky. The crescent moon lay on its back; the evening star flickered close by. He exhaled carefully as pieces of a puzzle tried to fall into place.

Confused, he turned around and walked slowly to the bed. He couldn't love her, could he? Feeling lightheaded, he sat down quickly and rubbed a hand over his face. He was being ridiculous. Love? Nah, pure, unadulterated lust was probably closer to the truth. She was a sexy, desirable woman and for the moment, at least, she seemed to like spending time with him. That was all.

He'd better try and get some sleep. Darryn had spoken about some event here the following morning that he'd organized to begin their advertising campaign for the new hotel. The previous night, Don had been far too busy making love to Caitlin to think about sleeping.

Just before he drifted off to sleep, he frowned. There it was again. That word.

Love.

CHAPTER 14

The phone was ringing when Caitlin opened the door to her rooms. Maggie was not there yet, so she lengthened her strides to answer. The ringing was not helping her headache. That was all she had to show for a day she'd spent waiting for a freaking phone call.

"This is Caitlin," she answered, more curtly than she normally would.

"Caitlin?" Don's voice sounded far away but it was him. He'd phoned her. She clutched the receiver with both hands and sat down quickly. Her legs felt a bit rubbery.

"Hi," she breathed like a lovesick schoolgirl.

"I'm sorry I didn't phone yesterday—"

"It doesn't matter," she interrupted him, because now that she was talking to him, it didn't matter in the least. He'd phoned. She was speaking to him.

He laughed. "I had a long explanation ready but if you don't want to hear it, fine by me," he said.

"How was your flight? And the meeting?"

"The flight was long, the meeting longer." There was a moment of silence. "I miss you," he said, his voice making her weak-kneed.

"I miss you too," she said softly, wondering if she'd be

heard over shouts in the background.

"Look, I'm sorry, but I have to go. Darryn has arranged some event here this morning and I have to be there. We don't have cell phone reception here. Do you have a landline at home?"

"No, but…"

"Okay, I'll try and phone tomorrow again. Got to go," he said and then the line was dead.

"And that smile?" Maggie asked as she walked through the door.

"A happy smile," Caitlin replied, grabbing her appointment book.

It was going to be a busy day, which was a good thing. She didn't want to have time to think too much about the fact that Don had, in fact, phoned her. That he'd said he missed her. A warm feeling opened up low in her belly. She was so, so happy.

***

"What the hell is wrong with you?" Darryn snarled. "You keep smiling like an idiot."

Don looked at Darryn and couldn't prevent another smile. They were standing outside, waiting for the arrival of a film crew and models Darryn had organized for the ad shoot.

"There, did you see that?" Darryn asked, turning to David and Dale. "He keeps smiling. We don't have anything to smile about yet."

"He probably had sex." David chuckled. "Something you obviously hadn't had for a while. You're in a filthy mood, brother," he said, and slapped Darryn on the shoulder.

Darryn turned to Don again and his eyes narrowed. "Did you?" he asked Don.

"Did I what?"

"Have sex."

"None of your damn business," Don said mildly.

Darryn frowned. "As long as it's not one of the Sutherland sisters…"

"What is wrong with the Sutherland sisters?" David asked. "They're beautiful and sexy. And I, for one, wouldn't mind having sex with any of them."

"As long as it's not Caitlin, you're welcome," Don said slowly as the truck with the film crew drew up.

David laughed out loud. "Told you he had sex."

"Maybe you should read her blog before you sleep with her again," Darryn mumbled.

"What blog?" Don asked.

"She has a blog. One of the sisters mentioned it. Read it. They all have serious issues," Darryn said and then people were tumbling out of vans and buses and there was no time to talk.

***

Caitlin was sitting on her couch, her legs tucked in under her. She was drinking a glass of wine and paging through a magazine. The television was on and she vaguely heard someone reading the latest news.

She'd had a busy day but nothing could spoil her buoyant mood. Don had phoned. What that meant or whether it meant anything at all was irrelevant at this point. She'd been floating on a cloud all day.

Something—a feeling, a voice—inside her was straining to be heard and she was trying very hard not to take notice. If she had to think about it, it had probably started somewhere between the time she had first touched Don's skin and their first kiss. She had been mostly unaware of it until today. Until his phone call.

What exactly it was, she wasn't ready to think about because then she would have to name this something. And she was afraid to do that. She knew with a deep certainty that this was like nothing she'd experienced before, this feeling wasn't something that was going to pass: it was too deep for that. And that freaked her out a little. She frowned. Okay, to be quite honest, it freaked her out a lot.

Her phone rang. It was Zoe.

"Hi, are you in Johannesburg already?" Caitlin asked.

"Are you watching the news?" Zoe's voice was strained.

Caitlin turned her head to look at the television only to see Don's smiling face covering the whole screen. Well, almost the whole screen. Because hanging on to his arm for dear life was a blonde. A tall, willowy blonde with not too much on.

A pain so sharp pierced through her body she had to bite back the automatic cry.

"I'm so sorry," Zoe whispered.

Caitlin had to swallow several times before she could talk. She tried to laugh but it didn't really work. "I've known all along that this wouldn't last. Remember, I told you. I just didn't think it would be quite so short-lived."

"Do you want me to phone Dana?" Zoe asked at the same moment her front door bell rang.

Like an automaton, Caitlin walked to the door and opened it.

"She's just arrived. Don't worry about me."

"Okay, great. I'm driving through to see Dale Cavallo and his brothers tomorrow. I'll be sure not to give Don your regards," she snapped.

"Zoe, please promise me you won't…" Caitlin began, but Zoe had already put the phone down.

Dana was closing the front door behind her. Caitlin stared at her. Everything that had happened over the last few minutes was registering bit by bit. And she knew. She'd made the same mistake her mother had made, the one mistake she'd promised herself she'd never make. She'd fallen in love with a man who couldn't be faithful.

"I love him, Dana," she said and burst into tears.

Dana opened her arms and Caitlin fell into them.

***

Don and his brothers were enjoying a long, cold beer when Zoe stopped in front of the guest house. He remembered that Dale had told them earlier she'd be doing the interior of the new hotel and would be arriving sometime that day. He'd phoned Caitlin's rooms early in the morning but the receptionist told him that Caitlin would not be in. Which was strange; she hadn't said anything the day before. A niggling feeling had been with him ever since.

They all stood up and he followed Dale when he walked toward the car. It wasn't Caitlin, but it was somehow nice to have her sister here. And maybe she'd know how he could get in touch with Caitlin and why she wasn't at her rooms today.

Zoe got out of the car. The look she sent in his direction was scorching.

What the hell?

"Hi, how was your drive?" Dale asked.

"Long," Zoe said tersely and closed the door.

Don pointed toward the boot. "Any luggage?" he asked, and she rounded on him.

"You!" she snarled. "I don't even know what to say to you! How could you hurt my sister like that?"

Don was completely taken aback. He looked at Dale for help, but his brother only shrugged, looking as perplexed as he was.

"I'm sorry but I don't know what you are talking about," he said, trying to stay calm.

Zoe threw him a shriveling look before she turned around and walked toward the house.

"Dale, could we start the meeting? I want to be back in Johannesburg tonight."

"But, you have a room here…" Dale began.

"I'm not staying under the same roof with

this…this…man," Zoe said angrily and pointed toward Don.

He quickly walked up to Zoe and took her arm. She tried to wriggle free but he held on tightly.

"What are you talking about?" he asked slowly.

Zoe pushed at him with one hand. "You have the gall to ask. Typical. You don't care how many broken hearts you leave behind you, as long as there is a blonde waiting around the next corner. Why would you care about hurting other people?" she cried out.

Don dropped her arm. David and Darryn had joined them. Don looked at his brothers. "Do you know what she's going on about?" he asked.

They all shrugged and looked at Zoe. She folded her arms and glared at them.

"Oh, now you don't remember the blonde who was plastered all over you?"

"What blonde?" his brothers asked simultaneously and they looked at one another.

Zoe rolled her eyes. "Your new hotel was on television last night, on the news channel. Don't tell me you didn't know. I don't care what went on here yesterday, but the clip they showed?" Zoe asked furiously. "Was of a blonde draped all over you." She spoke slowly and didn't take her eyes off Don. "And my sister saw that. You remember her? Caitlin? The one you spent a night with?"

Blonde? Television? News? Don was so baffled by Zoe's behavior it took him a while to process what she had said.

"Told you he had sex," David said under his breath. "We made an ad. That was what happened here yesterday," David said loudly.

"What blonde? What picture?" Darryn asked.

Don frowned and tried to remember what had happened the previous day. The film crew and models had been all over the place, but he and his brothers had been in meetings with the architects all morning. They only joined the others for lunch…

"The only time we saw the crew and models was during lunch," Darryn said.

"I didn't notice a camera nearby," Don said, still trying to sort out the sequence of yesterday's events. "Oh yes, now I remember. I'd just taken a plate to get lunch…"

"And I remember the blonde, now." Dale smiled.

"Of course you would," Zoe scowled.

"And she did kind of throw herself at you." David chuckled.

Don wanted to throttle his brothers. They were not helping.

He turned to Zoe. "Let me get this straight. There was a picture of a blond woman and myself on the news last night. And from that you and presumably your sister deduced that one, I'm having an affair with her and two, that I deliberately set out to hurt Caitlin. Is that what you're saying?" he asked through clenched teeth.

Zoe nodded once.

Don counted to ten. "The television camera was around. There were other people here. We were working. I don't even remember the blonde. You Sutherlands should get over your trust issues, damn it."

He turned to his brothers. "I'm out of here. Call me if you have a crisis," he said.

Darryn fell into step beside him. "I told you these sisters are trouble. Read her blog," he said before moving away.

***

Don read the last entry on Caitlin's blog and abruptly closed his laptop. He leaned back in his seat. It was late but he was on the company plane, heading back to Cape Town.

It had not been difficult to find Caitlin's writing. It was up on the internet, under her own name, out there for all to see. And he'd just read through entry after entry in which men were basically vilified. Granted, she and her sisters had obviously had some bad experiences with members of his sex but to write about members of his sex as if they all fitted nicely into one of a few categories was simply ridiculous. And sexist, if he wasn't mistaken.

The last entry had obviously been written after the first time he'd kissed her. Yes, he hadn't phoned, but he had warned her he might not be able to. And then she'd seen the picture in the newspaper. He did eventually explain the photo but was that something he wanted to do for the rest of his life?

She was obviously carrying a world of hurt and resentment with her. Now her mantra seemed to be: don't trust men, and it didn't seem as if she made any allowances. Could he change her mind? Did he want to?

He would try to talk to her one more time. He'd tried to call her the minute he had cell phone connection, but his calls had been ignored all day long.

What was it her mother had said? Their dad had left them and they all had trust issues. That was putting it mildly.

At this point he wasn't sure what to do next. He refused to keep explaining himself. Hell, he'd spent a night with Caitlin. How could she even think that he'd simply move on to the next woman the minute he'd left her?

Don stared out of the plane window. They were probably flying over the wide-open spaces of the Karoo, as there were very few lights down below. And looking down, he remembered the other thing Caitlin's mum had told him: the man who falls in love with any of them will have the difficult task of earning their trust. So he will have to make sure exactly what his feelings are.

Love. That word again. Time stood still for a moment. And then finally, those pieces of the puzzle he'd been ignoring for a while now fell neatly into place. He knew. Exactly.

He loved her. Don rubbed his hand over his face and shook his head. If his brothers could hear him now. But hell, he didn't care. He loved her. And he was sure she felt something for him, too. He knew enough about her to know she wouldn't have spent the night with him if she hadn't.

It was time for a plan. The big question now was how to get Caitlin to trust him? It was going to be a difficult task, as her mother had warned. But getting people to trust him was something he did every day. Surely he would be able to convince one sexy physiotherapist that he meant what he said?

Don grabbed his cell phone and looked through his diary. A plan. That was what was needed now. At least he now had a name for this weird feeling that had been with him ever since Caitlin had put her hands on his back. Stunned, he lifted his head. That was the moment he'd fallen for her. That was how long he'd been in love with her. The smile was back on his face.

CHAPTER 15

Caitlin drove home like a zombie. She'd gotten through one more day. That was good. That was progress. Wasn't it? As long as she was busy, she could ignore the constant pain that had been her companion since Monday night.

Don. The blonde. On television. How could he? How could he make love to her and then walk straight into the arms of that woman? He'd even phoned. Why? Because, dummy, he had not been making love to you, he'd had sex with you.

What had happened between them had been extraordinary for her, but for him she had been just another sucker who had fallen for his sexy smile. She was so angry with herself. Her own dad was an example of why she shouldn't trust a man. Ever.

But instead of listening to the voice in her head, she'd ignored it and had fallen in love with a man she'd known she would never be able to trust. Could one person be so stupid? And even worse, she couldn't get the wretched man out of her head.

Her whole body ached. She was miserable. She'd been crying herself to sleep for the last three nights like a medieval princess who had lost her knight. She pined for him. Damn it. She sniffled. This had to stop. Tonight.

As she made the turn into the street where she lived, she saw Don's car in front of her house and her heart skipped a beat before it sank. Just when she'd decided to get over him. For a minute she considered turning around and driving away, but then she squared her shoulders.

This was her street, her house. And he was not welcome here. She drove slowly closer and when she parked, he got out of his car.

She grabbed her laptop and the few groceries she'd bought. Before she could open her door, though, he was there.

"Hi," he said and took the groceries from her.

She tried to hold on to the bag, but he just smiled and she let go.

"Key?" He held out his hand.

"Don, what are you doing here?" she asked, fed up with the whole situation.

"I want to speak to you," he said. "Key?"

"Well, I don't want to speak to you," she just about snarled and walked around him to the front door.

"Pity. But maybe a good thing." He followed her up the steps.

She whipped out the key and glared at him. He took it from her and opened the door. Head held high, she walked into the house and put her laptop and handbag down on the nearest table.

"Why is it a good thing?" she asked, irritated.

He smiled. "Then you can listen," he said slowly and walked closer to her.

"To what? More lies?" she hissed.

He put the groceries down on the table.

"I've never lied to you," he said quietly.

"You had sex with me the one night and the next day you were with someone else. That's not lying?" she asked.

He took her hands in his. She tried to break free, but he held on tightly.

"Let me go," she snapped while trying to pull away.

"No," he said emphatically, then pulled her closer.

Caitlin stopped her struggling and looked up at him. There were shadows under his eyes and he hadn't shaved for a few days. She looked away. It was too painful to have him here, to have his scent surrounding her and to know she could never again trust him.

He folded his hand over both of hers and trapped them against his body. His heartbeat was unsteady under her fingers. With his other hand, he lifted her chin.

"I want you to look at me when I say this," he said his eyes nearly black. "I can explain every single move I make every single day, but I can't live like that. No one can live like that. You have to trust me."

"How can you say that? How can I trust you when—"

"Because I love you," he said and pulled her closer still.

Dumbfounded, Caitlin stared at him for a moment before she laughed.

"Oh, you love me. Of course. That would explain why you spend one night with me and the next with someone else?" She didn't bother to hide the sarcasm.

"Yes, I love you," he said. "And that should explain why you should know that I would never do that."

Caitlin looked into his eyes. He seemed sincere: he was here, touching her, telling her he loved her.

"I have to travel a lot and I don't want to have to explain every silly woman who wants to be in a picture with me. You have to be able to trust me."

There was a ravine gaping right in front of her. She could take the step to cross it, but what if she missed and fell?

She shook her head. "I…Don, it's not easy for me, I…"

He stepped back. "I know. Your mother told me about your dad—"

"When?" she interrupted him.

His smile was lopsided. "On Mahé. I think she knew

how I felt about you even before I realized it myself."

Caitlin shook her head trying to make sense of what he was saying. Had he loved her way back then?

He tapped on her laptop. "And I've read your blog."

"Really? I haven't written anything for a while, not since…"

Don nodded. "Not since you neatly filed me under the category of the-ones-who-never-phone-again."

"You're angry about that."

"I'm pi—ticked off that you made wild assumptions about me. And that you continue to do so."

Caitlin didn't know what to say. She should believe him. He took the trouble to come to her house, to talk to her. To tell her he loved her. And she wanted to tell him she loved him back, but something was holding her back, preventing her from uttering the words.

Don grabbed her hand and pulled her closer.

"I love you. I'm in love with you. And I've never said that to another woman."

She moved away from him and clutched her hands together. He couldn't love her. He was a Cavallo: rich, powerful. They mixed with celebrities from around the world. And she was just…

"Yes? You're just?" Don asked and turned her back to face him.

She had to have spoken the words out loud. But maybe that was a good thing.

"I'm just a physio from a small town. I…"

There was an ache in her throat, making it impossible to speak.

He was breathing heavily and his nostrils had turned white. He was angry, she realized.

"So you've managed to find one more reason not to be with me." His voice was cool, but his eyes… He couldn't be hurt, could he?

Don cupped her face. "I love you. And yes, I'm rich, I'm not apologizing for that. I work very hard for what I have. You can probably come up with more excuses why we shouldn't be together. I can't change your mind, Caitlin. Only you have the power to either believe me, believe in us, or not."

He bent down and kissed her. Passionately. Then he turned around and walked to the front door.

"Lock the door behind me. And let me know what you decide," he said and then he was gone.

Caitlin sagged down on the nearest chair and stared at the door. Lock the door, he'd said. That was the easy part. It was the let-me-know-what-you-decide part she didn't know how to do.

A big hole was opening up inside of her. She felt drained, empty. So, so empty.

Her phone rang and she jumped up and searched through her bag. Would Don…? Her heart beat frantically while she took it out. But it was her mother.

"Hi, Mum," she said, trying to sound normal.

"Caitlin?" her mother asked. "What's wrong?"

Caitlin swallowed. "Nothing's wrong. Are you at home? I was thinking of coming over for a glass of wine."

"Great! That's why I called. I've tried a new chicken recipe…"

"Say no more, I'm on my way," Caitlin said and grabbed her bag.

***

"I want to ask you something, Mum," Caitlin said.

They had just finished their dinner and were sitting on the front veranda of her mother's house. It was a beautiful December evening. The sun was just disappearing below the horizon and the last rays had draped the bay in hues of soft pink.

"I'm listening."

"I want to know about Dad…"

"Oh, sweetheart, you should put the past behind you,

I—"

"I want to, but I have to understand why," Caitlin said.

Her mother looked at her. "Why now?"

"Because…" Caitlin stopped. She wasn't ready to talk about Don yet. "I just want to know," she said. "He married you, you had his children. Presumably he loved you, loved us. So how could he just walk away?"

Her mother sighed before she looked out over the bay. "We married very young, straight out of university. We had no idea what love really meant. We liked each other, we had fun together and kind of drifted into marriage. It was never a conscious decision. Then we had you girls within the first four years of our marriage. I regret many things, but never that. And then…" She shrugged. "I grew up quickly, he didn't. And in a sense, I don't think he ever will. That's part of his charm, I suppose, who he is." She smiled. "I liked your dad, and I loved him, dearly. I still do. But like a friend, you know? And he realized that long before I did. He loves you girls, though, in his way."

She laughed. "He is not marriage material, never was, never will be. But you must never make the mistake of thinking all men are like him. And as you know, I still believe in love. That's why I write about it."

"So, how do you know?" Caitlin asked. "How do you know that what you feel is the right kind of love?"

"Do you feel something for someone?" her mother asked with a smile.

Caitlin nodded. "But he has money, he's from such a different world. I don't know how I'd fit into it."

Her mother smiled. "If you believe that, you don't give me or yourself enough credit. Whether you have money or not doesn't determine who you are." She leaned forward and touched Caitlin's hand. "Listen to your heart, Caitlin, trust what you feel. I didn't." She kissed Caitlin's forehead. "You'll do the right thing, I know. Just don't let the guy get away while you're worrying about stuff like money. There is nothing sadder than that."

Caitlin squeezed her mother's hand. Emotion had clogged up her throat. She couldn't speak.

"Now, let's talk about Christmas," her mother said, changing the subject.

"What's to talk about?" Caitlin asked. "Aren't we doing our usual thing? Just us girls and lots and lots of food?"

"I wanted to make sure you didn't have other plans. I've spoken to the others. Zoe doesn't have a problem and Dana will join us, her mum is visiting her brother in Dubai, but Hannah might not make it."

"Why?" Caitlin asked, frowning. "I thought she was coming back this weekend. That's what she told me on Saturday. Christmas is only next Wednesday. She'll be in time."

"She has some problem with her flight. But she'll let us know by tomorrow."

***

Caitlin was trying to fall asleep when she became aware of it. The dull ache she'd been carrying around with her over the last few days was gone. In its place something warm had nestled close to her heart. Hannah would probably tell her it was just indigestion. She smiled.

Trust your heart, her mother had said. Don had said he loved her. She knew that what she felt for him was so intense, so different from anything else she'd experienced before, it could only be love. But was that enough? To trust him?

Don never did explain about the woman on his arm, she realized just before she fell asleep. Strange, it didn't seem to bother her so much at this point. But she was floating away on a cloud. Maybe she'd be upset again tomorrow.

CHAPTER 16

Caitlin took a sip of her coffee. She'd left Hermanus early that morning and was waiting for her father. She'd phoned him the previous night to ask if they could meet.

After the talk she'd had with her mother Thursday evening, the anger and resentment she'd felt toward her father had somehow started to diminish. It was as if a huge burden she'd been carrying around with her for all these years had miraculously been lifted from her shoulders.

He was her dad and it was time to let him back into her life. A part of her would always be sad that he'd left them, but her mother had forgiven him a long time ago and had moved on with her life. It was time she did the same.

Don had told her he'd read through her blog. So, over the last couple of nights, she'd read through everything she'd written. And that was when it had dawned on her.

Yes, many of the guys she'd been out with had been terrible dates, but she'd been looking for a flaw. The poor men never had a chance; she'd put them in one of her categories without a second thought. And each time she'd written them off as bad dates, she'd been feeding the hurt and anger her father's leaving had left inside of her.

Don had told her he loved her, had asked her to trust

him. And it should have been the easiest thing to do. But she couldn't. She'd let him walk out of her house. Because she was scared. Because she could be hurt again.

She loved him. Loved him in a way she hadn't known was possible. But all the what-ifs she could think of had been spinning through her head since he'd told her. She wanted to believe him, wanted to trust him, wanted desperately to tell him how she felt, but something was holding her back.

And during another sleepless night, she'd realized that she would have to let go of the hurt her father had caused. This was why she was here. Hopefully, talking to him would help her make sense of things and she'd be able to find closure.

She looked around her. The Waterfront in Cape Town was obviously a tourist favorite and the whole place was overflowing with people. Babies were crying, people were talking, street musicians were making music and it sounded to her as if the noise level rose by the minute. The vibe was contagious and she smiled. It was two days before Christmas, and the festive feeling was in the air.

"Hi, baby girl." She heard her father's voice and turned around as he planted a quick kiss on her cheek.

"Hi. Thanks for meeting me."

The tall, still attractive man who was her father sat down next to her. He'd grown old, she realized. He still looked good for someone his age, but his hair was thinning and his chin was sagging. He was always so full of life. She'd never thought of him as getting old.

He called a waiter over and ordered another coffee before he sat down. "So, what brings you all the way from Hermanus?"

"Shopping," Caitlin said after a beat.

"Lovely shops they have here, I know." He smiled and thanked the waiter for the coffee he put down in front of him.

"How are your sisters?" he asked.

"Well, Hannah is still in Paris. We hope she'll be home in time for Christmas, and Zoe…"

Caitlin stopped talking and stared at her father. He wasn't listening to her; he was looking past her and was winking at someone.

She turned around. An older woman with bottle-blond hair, wearing a dress a few sizes too small, was sitting just behind them and was clearly flirting with her father.

Open-mouthed, she turned back to him. He laughed when he saw her face.

"What? She's a beautiful woman, It's a beautiful day."

Caitlin wanted to be angry, wanted to say something bitchy, but it seemed so silly somehow. She laughed. Her mother was so right. He'd never grown up. And for the first time she saw that and accepted it.

"Can I ask you something?" she asked, still smiling.

Warily, he looked at her. "Personal?"

"Yes, it's personal. Why did you marry Mum?"

He looked away for a moment. "Your mother was the love of my life. But I wasn't the right man for her." Briefly, there was a hint of sadness in his eyes but then he laughed and the twinkle was back. "And there are all these other women." He winked at her and spread his hands in the air. "What's a man to do?"

"Stay faithful?" she asked, but without the usual malice.

"Not in my nature, baby girl, I'm afraid, not in my nature." He smiled. He picked up her hand. "But I do love you and your sisters. I've never been much of a father to you girls, but never doubt that."

"I know." Caitlin stood up. "Thanks for meeting me…Dad." She smiled and bent down to kiss him.

Walking away, she felt lighter somehow. It had always been difficult for her to call him anything, let alone Dad. But, she glanced back and smiled, he was her father, warts and all. He had joined the bottle blonde in the too-tight dress.

She would never really understand him but then she

didn't have to. Her mother had been right about something else as well. Not all men were like her father.

Don was so different to her father. Caitlin remembered her last date with Don. His gaze had never left hers. He hadn't looked around and tried to catch someone else's eye: he had been interested only in her.

And then there was the way he'd looked after them on Mahé. She hadn't wanted to see it like that, but he had taken care of them. He'd gone out of his way to make sure they were as comfortable as possible, given the circumstances.

He and his brothers had made sure they stayed in one of their hotels. He'd personally driven them around when there were probably a million other urgent things that had to be done. And he'd even thought ahead and arranged the car for them at the airport.

He'd shown her he loved her even before he'd realized it himself.

The words of the song playing over the loudspeakers penetrated her thoughts. She recognized it as one of the songs by a well-known country rock group.

Humming the well-known tune, she paused mid-stride. The lyrics raced around her brain. She looked up to the clear blue sky and smiled. Of course. Love only comes once in a while. And for her, that love was Don.

A contentment she'd never known before settled over her and she ran up the steps to where her car was parked. At this point, she still didn't have all the answers she'd been looking for but that didn't seem to be so important right now.

It was nearly Christmas. Her rooms were closed for the next two weeks. Zoe would arrive in Hermanus that day. Hopefully, Hannah would be on time and they'd start with all the preparations for Christmas.

That meant she had three days in which to decide how she was going to tell Don she loved him.

***

"Tell me," Don's mother said, and he smiled. Trust her not to miss a thing. She'd been staring at him all through lunch. His dad and brothers had wandered out to the garden at the back of his mother's restaurant, leaving him alone with her at the table.

"Tell you what?" he stalled.

"Something happened to you. I can see that. Tell me," she said again.

Don smiled. "You know I'm nearly thirty-four?"

"You're still my son. Tell me," she insisted and moved her chair closer to his.

She peered into his face.

"Mum, really, I…"

She touched his face and smiled. "I see. You love her."

He barked out a laugh. He never could fool his mother.

"So? What's the problem?"

"She has…trust issues," he said.

"So? What's the problem?" his mother insisted.

"What problem?" his father asked as he and Don's brothers strolled in.

"No problem," Don said and got up.

"I'm off," Darryn said and kissed their mother.

They all said goodbye and moved toward the door. Don hung back. He had something else he had to tell his mother and would rather do it after his brothers had left.

"By the way," David said as they all reached the front door, "I won't be here for Christmas lunch."

Surprised, Don looked at his brother's retreating back. That was what he'd wanted to talk to his mother about as well.

"Me neither," said Darryn, who waved before he stepped out of the restaurant.

"I also have a thing," Dale mumbled and left.

His mother turned to face him, a small smile playing around her lips. "And you, Donato? You also have a thing?"

"I…" He cleared his throat. "I also won't make it this year," he said and waited for her to explode.

But she only shrugged. "Oh, okay," she said.

"I thought you'd be upset," he said, puzzled. Usually his mother was very insistent that if at all possible, they should be together for Christmas lunch.

"Why would I be upset? You're all grown men," she said.

He listened carefully to try and detect any reproach in her voice, but she genuinely seemed to accept the fact that none of her sons would be spending Christmas with the family.

"Well, fine then. I'll stop by on Tuesday before I leave."

"Looking forward to it," his mother said before she kissed him. "And about that problem you have? Fix it. That's what you do all day, you fix problems. Fix this one too."

***

Caitlin was excited. And nervous. But more excited. Tomorrow was Christmas. She'd spend the day with her mother, her sisters, and Dana, and then on Thursday she'd phone Don. The exact how, when, and where she was still trying to figure out but she wanted to tell him how she felt.

She grabbed her keys. Hannah's plane should be landing in about two hours. There was a point when it didn't look as if Hannah would be home in time, but she'd phoned late yesterday to say she had been able to get a ticket.

Caitlin glanced at her watch. Good, she had enough time to also make a quick stop at the shopping mall. There was something she wanted to get. She grinned. She couldn't wait to see Don's face when she gave it to him.

***

"You look completely stressed out. Hannah, what is going on?" Caitlin asked urgently and sat down next to her sister. The minute they'd entered Caitlin's house, Hannah had sat down on her couch and was lying with her head against the cushions.

She'd waited for Hannah outside the airport building and because it had been dark already she hadn't really looked at her sister until they'd walked into Caitlin's house. Her usually poised and calm sister was pale and she looked exhausted. Something was very wrong.

Hannah opened one eye. "Not tonight, please. I'll talk to you all after our Christmas lunch, I promise."

"Okay, I'm going to run you a bath," Caitlin, leaning forward to rise. She would have liked to help Hannah but it was clear that she'd have to wait to hear what was wrong.

Her sister patted the seat next to her. "Not before you tell me what happened to you? You're lit up like a Christmas tree."

Caitlin smiled and sat down. "Oh, so you don't have to talk but I do?"

"I have a not-so-nice story. You, on the other hand, are glowing. So I assume you have a happy story?"

Caitlin laughed. "I do. I've been dying to tell someone, but Mum has been running around like a headless chicken organizing this Christmas lunch, Dana only finished teaching today and was busy with final marks, and Zoe and you have been away. Zoe only came back yesterday and has still been in Cape Town."

"Don Cavallo?" Hannah asked, eyebrow raised.

Caitlin nodded, the smile nearly splitting her face in two. "I know you think it's a mistake, but Hannah, he told me he loves me!" she cried out.

Hannah sat up and took one of her hands. "And you? How do you feel about him?"

"I love him, Hannah. So much." Caitlin sighed and pressed her hands against her heart.

Hannah stared at her. "You know they are rich. Very, very rich. They lead completely different lives to us. He will be away all the time. Are you ready for that?"

"I know, Hannah, I know. But I also know that what I feel I've never felt before and I might never feel again." She smiled. "And I'm getting used to this idea of a rich boyfriend."

They giggled.

"Zoe told me about the picture of him and a blonde on the news. How did he explain that?" asked Hannah.

"He didn't and it doesn't matter. I…" She laughed. "I never thought these words would come out of my mouth, but I trust him."

"And? What did he say?"

"I haven't told him yet. I…" Caitlin jumped up. "I don't even know if he's in the country at the moment, but I'm going to phone him after our Christmas thing. I wanted to talk to you guys first."

"So Mum and Zoe don't know yet?" Hannah asked and also got up from the couch.

"I think Mum suspects but I haven't spoken to Zoe yet. Last time she and I spoke she was so angry with him. She's staying with Mum tonight. We can all have our confessions tomorrow after lunch."

"So? When's the date?"

"What date?" Caitlin asked, puzzled.

"The wedding date?"

"What wed…? Oh, you're talking about Don and me…" Stunned, Caitlin stared at Hannah. "No, he…I…" She shook her head. "I don't think that's on the table, Hannah."

"And you're okay with that?" Hannah asked.

Caitlin thought for a moment. "I'm okay with that. Whether I have a ring on my finger or not, it won't change the way I feel about him."

"Then I'm happy for you. Truly. But he has to know. If he messes with my big sister, I mess with him." Hannah smiled and hugged her.

Caitlin stood up and took Hannah's arm. "Look at you. You can hardly stand up straight. No messing around with anyone tonight."

Later, as she lay listening to the waves crashing against the rocks, she thought about Hannah's remark again. Wedding. Marriage. Babies. She could see little ones playing on the lawn. She smiled and drifted away. Little boys with chocolate brown eyes.

CHAPTER 17

"Hi everyone!" Caitlin called as she, Dana, and Hannah entered her mother's house. They had their hands full of presents.

No one answered, but they could hear voices coming from inside—Zoe's was the loudest.

"Dining room," Hannah said, starting down the corridor.

"Zoe sounds upset," Caitlin said, following her.

"I honestly don't know why you didn't tell me," Zoe was saying as they entered the dining room. "Does Caitlin know?"

"Know what?" Caitlin asked as she put her presents around the tree.

"That the whole Cavallo clan will be here for lunch," Zoe said, pointing to the dining room table.

Caitlin straightened and looked at the table. The table was laid for six extra people. Her heart skipped a beat before it began a cheerful dance. For a minute, she felt lightheaded and clutched the back of one of the chairs.

"See?" Zoe said triumphantly. "You've upset Caitlin, too. The last person she wants to see today is Don Cavallo. Tell her, Caitlin," Zoe said heatedly.

Hannah walked over to her mother and hugged her. "Hi, Mum," she said and looked over her shoulder at the table. "Exactly how many of the Cavallos have you invited?" she asked coolly.

"All of them. And no one is upset, Zoe, except you." Caitlin's mother turned to Caitlin. "You're not upset, Caitlin, are you?"

Caitlin didn't know whether to laugh or cry. She'd had a plan. She was going to phone Don that night and was going to see him tomorrow. There was going to be enough time to think about what she was going to say to him. She'd have time to inform the rest of her family about her change of heart.

And now he was going to be here. At her mother's house. On Christmas Day. She laughed out loud.

"Mum!" she cried, hugging first her mother and then a frowning Zoe. "I'm not upset in the least. In fact, I was going to wait until after lunch but I have something to tell all of you," she said, completely out of breath.

Her mother beamed. "Before you say anything, I'm getting a bottle of bubbly!" She laughed and clapped her hands. "I have a very good idea what you want to tell us. Dana, get the glasses!" she called over her shoulder as she hurried in the direction of the kitchen. "This is going to be a wonderful, wonderful story, I can't wait to start writing…"

With a worried look on her face, Zoe took Caitlin's hand. "The last time I spoke to you, you were crying over Don Cavallo. We were both angry with him. What has happened since then?"

"That's what I want to know as well," Dana said while taking glasses out of a cupboard. "We didn't like this Don. Then you had a date and we liked him. Then something happened and we didn't like him. Then you had another date and we liked him again. But then another thing happened and we stopped liking him. And now…?"

Caitlin laughed out loud. "We like him. But let's first

get some bubbly into you guys. You are way too tense for this beautiful day. It's Christmas, guys, anything is possible!"

Her mother came in, still smiling and holding a bottle of bubbly in her hand. "I agree! Isn't it wonderful? I'll pour, you talk," she said and pointed to Caitlin.

***

Don checked his GPS again before he turned into the street. This was a lovely part of Hermanus. The houses on this side of the road all had a spectacular view of the bay.

He couldn't remember the last time he'd been so excited to go to a Christmas lunch. He and his brothers owned some of the most glamorous and smart boutique hotels one could find. There had definitely been more glitzy Christmas parties in the past, parties at arguably more exotic places, but if he had to choose, there was nowhere on earth he'd rather be than here today.

Even though the whole thing was messing with his plans.

He had been going to keep his distance until Caitlin contacted him, or at least, he had been going to try. But when her mother had phoned to invite him to their Christmas lunch, he'd accepted without a second thought.

He'd be close to Caitlin. Where he wanted to be. Even if she didn't believe him or trust him. Hell, he missed her. He missed everything about her but mostly he missed the way she made him feel. When he was with her, everything was brighter, better.

Precisely how everything was going to work out, he wasn't sure. Which was a first for him. Usually he liked to know all the odds, but for once it didn't really matter.

He wasn't even sure she'd be glad to see him, but her mother had invited him. For Christmas lunch. That had to mean something, right? He'd have preferred to be alone with her somewhere, but he'd have to tell her family at some point that he loved her and maybe Christmas Day was as good a day as any.

Don drove slowly down the street, checking numbers on both sides of the road. There was a slight bend ahead and it was only when he'd passed it that he looked in front of him again.

He stepped on the brakes. And stared. Because parked on both sides of the street in front of a lovely white house with a green roof were his brothers' cars. The three of them were standing in front of the gate, looking in his direction. What the hell? He drove closer and parked behind Darryn.

As he crossed the street, someone called his name from behind. He turned around in time to see his parents getting out of their car.

Darryn swore.

"Well, this explains a lot." David chuckled.

"Yeah. Why Mum didn't freak out when we told her we wouldn't be with them for Christmas. She's known all along," Dale said.

"I saw them yesterday," Don added, unable to hold back a grin. "They didn't say a word."

His dad called them over. "Come and help, please. Your mother has brought her whole restaurant with us."

***

Feminine giggles floated down the stairs.

Don's heart kicked up a notch. He grinned. "It sounds as if the party has started without us."

"I still want to know why we're all here," grumbled Darryn.

"You manage a multimillion-dollar business," his mum said with a smile in Darryn's direction. "I'm sure you'll be able to figure it out. Eventually."

"But…" Darryn began, frowning.

"Did anyone force you to come here today?" his

mother asked.

"That's not the point," Darryn began hotly.

"Do you want to be anywhere else?" his mother asked.

He opened his mouth but closed it again.

"Thought so." She smiled. "Now, smile boys, it's Christmas," she said and pressed the front doorbell.

***

He's here. Caitlin lifted her head just before the doorbell rang.

"I'll get the guests, you sit down and look pretty," their mother sang and hurried to the front door.

"Like a bloody scene from *Pride and Prejudice*," Zoe grumbled, but combed her fingers through her hair.

Dana giggled. "You could be making hats," she said, and they all burst into laughter.

Once they'd started, Caitlin couldn't stop. They'd had enough bubbly to make even Zoe's frown disappear. And anyway, none of them could ever stay mad for long.

"Mum wanted Don here for you, Caitlin, I get that," Hannah said. "He declared his love for you, you love him, etcetera, etcetera. But why did she invite all the other brothers?"

"That's what I want to know as well," Zoe said.

"Maybe she knows something you don't." Caitlin smiled. In her case, her mother had definitely figured out how she felt about Don long before she'd been sure herself.

The next moment the room was filled with Cavallos and her mother's sitting room looked much smaller than usual.

Caitlin nodded and smiled in the general direction of everyone but had eyes only for Don. When he met her gaze, he smiled back and she melted.

Wow. Seeing Caitlin here, smiling as if a light had been lit up inside of her literally took his breath away. For a few seconds everything else seemed to fade away and they were the only two people in the room.

She was wearing a short, loosely fitted white dress. The thin straps that seemed to be all that kept the dress from pooling at her feet left her shoulders bare. He dropped his gaze down to her legs. And desire slammed into him, leaving his mouth dry.

"Put the food down, son," his dad said, grinning.

Blinking, Don put the tray down on the nearest table.

Caitlin's mum hugged them all and he got a kiss on the cheek.

"So glad you're here," her mother whispered.

The three other women didn't come closer but nodded coolly in the Cavallos' direction.

And then Caitlin was there.

"Hi, Mr. Cavallo." She greeted his dad first and then she touched Don's arm.

"Bring the tray into the kitchen. I'll show you where it is." She smiled and he gladly followed her.

He had to get his hands on her. Soon.

"As you probably know by now, I don't cook. Do you know if we should heat this…?" Caitlin began.

But he put the tray down, turned her around, and kissed her.

"Don!" his mother called from the other room and Caitlin pushed him away, smiling.

"Where can we have some privacy?" he asked, trying to rein in his raging hormones.

"Don, I…" she began but he saw another door leading from the kitchen and pushed her through it into what looked like a scullery.

He closed the door behind them.

Caitlin gasped. "We can't stay here, there are…" she tried to say but he stopped her in the quickest way he could think of. He kissed her.

And this time he made sure she forgot about other people and other things. He knew he only had a few minutes so he put everything into that kiss—the depth of his love, the intensity of his desire, the urgency of his need for her.

Her arms crept around his neck and she melted against him.

Someone knocked on the door. Reluctantly, he lifted his head and brushed her hair away.

"Please put me out of my misery, I have to know. Just tell me..." he began but she was also speaking.

"I love you..."

"What did you say?" he asked, not daring to believe what he'd heard.

Caitlin laughed and pulled his head down. "I love you. I was going to phone you tonight and make plans to come and see you but my mother interfered and now you're here, but I want you to know that I was going to—"

"You had me at 'I love you.'" He smiled and placed a thumb over her lips. "No need to explain anything else. I was also going to phone you tonight and I think both our mothers interfered."

"Hey, Don!" David called from inside.

"Just a minute!" Don growled. He cupped Caitlin's face. "I hope you don't have any other plans later today, because I'm going home with you."

"We have to talk, I want to explain..." she began, but he kissed her again.

"I'm going home with you. And I don't want to talk," he said.

She nodded, her eyes glittering and for the first time in days he felt himself relax. It would seem he'd won the girl.

CHAPTER 18

Caitlin couldn't stop smiling. When they'd returned from the scullery, Don hadn't said anything, but he'd kept his hand in hers and with a pleased grin, taken his place next to her at the long table.

She was also glad to see that her sisters and Dana had relaxed enough to at least look as if they were having a good time. Her mother had put Darryn next to Hannah, Dale next to Zoe, and David next to Dana. Caitlin had been worried that there might be trouble but so far everyone seemed happy enough. Hannah was even talking to Darryn, which surprised her a little.

They'd just finished lunch. Caitlin was acutely aware of Don next to her. He'd kept touching her all through lunch and by now every single one of her nerve endings was over-stimulated. She couldn't wait to be alone with him but didn't want to be the first to get up.

"How are you getting back to Cape Town, Hannah?" Zoe asked. "I'm going back tomorrow if you want to wait until then."

"If you want to, you could go back with me this afternoon," David said.

Darryn glared in his direction. "I'll drive her," he

growled.

Hannah shook her head. "I'm staying with my mother for a few days, but thanks."

Don's mother leaned forward and looked at him, her eyes twinkling. "And Donato, are you staying here or driving back?" she asked.

Don smiled and got up. "I'm taking Caitlin home now, Mother."

"Oh," she said and lifted her eyebrows.

Don just smiled and touched Caitlin's shoulder. "Mrs. Sutherland, I'm taking Caitlin home now, if it's all right? We'll get her car later."

Her mother smiled. "Of course you are, dear." She got up. "I'm so glad you were here."

Then everyone was getting up and saying goodbye. Caitlin's mum gave her a fierce hug.

"Call me," she whispered quickly before Don steered her outside.

***

Caitlin waited for Don on the steps of her house. This time she handed the keys over gladly. There was no way she would be able to unlock the front door. Excitement, desire, need—all were raging through her body, making her feverish.

And then he came up the stairs and was there, right in front of her, his eyes dark with a look in them that instantly weakened her knees.

Without saying anything, he took the key and opened the door. She walked past him and put her bag down.

"Do you want anything?" she asked, walking toward the kitchen. "I'll get something, then we can talk…" was as far as she got.

Don grabbed her hand and pulled her back to him.

"What is it with you and talking?" he asked as he skimmed his hands down her body. "I don't want to talk and all I want is you," he said clearly. He paused for a last long look, and then slipped the straps of her dress over her shoulders.

He bent down and brushed his lips over her naked skin. "I've been dying to do this all day," he whispered.

"What?"

"This," he said, and pushed the straps down so that her dress dropped from her body and pooled at her feet. All she was wearing was a strapless lace bra and a tiny pair of white lace panties.

"Beautiful, so beautiful," he said in wonder and she felt like the most desirable woman on earth. He cupped her breasts with both hands and before she could catch her breath, he dropped down on his knees.

"Don!" she cried out.

He gathered her close, pressing his face into her body, his hands not quite steady. She tried to support herself by holding on to his shoulders. Her legs turned to rubber.

"I want to make love to you," he said and pushed the lace barrier down to leave her exposed to his hungry eyes. "All of you," he said and put his mouth where her whole body was screaming for him.

She tried to focus on him, on the muscles straining under his shirt, the hair curling around his collar, but she was spun out of control with the first flick of his tongue. This was too much, too much, she wanted to cry, but she couldn't form the words and he continued his onslaught until she sobbed out his name and sagged to the floor next to him.

***

She only remembered much later.

Don was snoring lightly but she knew that if she were to touch him, she'd be under him in two seconds flat. He was insatiable. And, she sighed, so was she. The moon was full, the beams fell through the window, lighting up the room. She crawled out of bed. It was time she showed him what a lovely Christmas present she'd bought him. It was still under the Christmas tree in her lounge.

A few minutes later, she was back. Don had turned on to his stomach, one arm flung sideways. Perfect. Exactly the position she wanted him in.

Caitlin slowly crawled over the bed and straddled him. Don stopped snoring and lifted his head.

"Caitlin?" he asked drowsily.

"You can go right back to sleep," she crooned and poured the fragrant oil on her palms. "I've bought you a Christmas present," she said and brought her hands down on his back. "It's massage oil and it has magic powers, I'm told." She continued to speak in even tones while she started kneading his shoulders.

"I don't have the words to tell you how much I love you, but I hope to show you," she said softly and he turned his head and looked at her.

He didn't say anything and she continued her massage. Soon, she was unaware of anything else but the movement of her hands, the solidity of his body, the unevenness of his breathing.

This time, there was nothing to prevent her from touching him everywhere. She loved the feel of his muscles flexing under her fingers and she massaged and stroked and rubbed every centimeter of his back until he was pliant and warm under her touch.

But she wasn't finished. Not nearly. She moved so that she sat beside him and her hands found their way down to his buttocks. No barrier prevented her from touching the hard muscles. His breath hitched in his throat but Caitlin continued touching him, working his backside and back. And each time her hands moved over his sides, they moved a little farther under his body.

She smiled and reached over him to pour more oil on her palms. The next minute, she was lying under him.

"Don!" she yelped and laughed.

But then he moved against her and her smile disappeared. He was hard and ready for her.

"This is what you do to me, what you did to me way back then," he said slowly while he became part of her. "And this is how much I love you," he whispered as he picked up the pace.

Caitlin tried to hold his gaze but passion clouded her vision and she threw her head back and lifted her body to meet his.

***

Don leaned on his elbow and stared at Caitlin. It was still early but the sun was up already and the rays fell on her, making her whole body glimmer. They did eventually make it to her bed. He put out a hand and touched her shoulder in wonder.

She loved him. Him. Not his money, not his possessions, not his hotels, not his cars. She'd told him all through the night—with her body, her voice, her hands. He wasn't sure how many times he'd turned to her during the night, but she'd always been ready for him, always welcoming.

And she'd stunned him with the massage. At that point he hadn't thought he had more to give, but the minute she'd touched him, his body went up in flames.

Another thought popped up out of nowhere. And once it was lodged in his mind, he couldn't think why it had taken him so long to realize this was what he'd wanted. What he'd wanted since the first moment he'd seen her. Because she hadn't only touched his body, she'd captivated his heart. Right from the beginning.

He put his hand out to wake her, to tell her, but stopped. Caitlin was still sleeping deeply. Quietly, he slipped out of bed. He was reluctant to leave her, but there was something else he had to do and he didn't want to wait.

***

Caitlin woke slowly. Her body was sore. No wonder. After a night like last night…

She smiled and turned her head, but Don wasn't next to her. She listened but couldn't hear any other sounds. He probably went out to get something to eat, she thought as she got up. Food had been the last thing on her mind last night but now she was also hungry.

She jumped out of bed and her gaze fell on her computer. Her blog. She smiled. She was finally able to write about the one empty category on her blog. The category of "the one." That would probably be her last entry. Because she'd found her perfect date at last. And this date was one she would hopefully be able to keep around for a long time.

And she knew exactly how to describe him. She would start with the way he'd looked back at her when she was looking at him.

She giggled, spun around, and hugged herself. While she was waiting for him, she'd have a shower and make coffee. Last time she checked, she had coffee at least. She stretched and walked to the bathroom.

The hot water was bliss. She put out a hand for the bar of soap just as the shower door opened behind her.

"There you are," she said and turned into Don's arms. "I missed you," she said and rose up to her toes.

He lifted an eyebrow. "Not worried that I'd skipped town?"

He was smiling but she sensed his uncertainty.

"No. You told me you loved me. I trust you," she said and slipped her arms around his neck. And blinked. She brushed his hair away from his forehead. "I actually mean that. I didn't really know until I said it, but I do. I do trust you," she said and kissed him.

"A good thing, because I have something to discuss

158

with you," he said formally while pulling her closer.

"Oh, is that what we're going to call this now? A discussion?" she asked and lifted her leg over his side.

"I…" He groaned and moved so that her back was against the wall. "Oh damn…later," he whispered. "We'll talk later."

Talking was also the last thing she wanted to do at that moment.

***

She was making coffee when her phone rang. Don was still in the bedroom.

It was her mother. Shaking her head, she answered. "Good morning, Mum."

"And?" her mother asked.

"And what?" Caitlin asked as she felt Don's arms circling her from behind.

He took her phone. "Good morning, Brenda. No, we haven't spoken yet. I promise you, you'll be the first to know." He chuckled and hung up the phone.

"Know what?" Caitlin asked, reaching up to take the coffee mugs down.

"When the wedding will be," he said and turned her around to face him.

"Wedding?" she asked, puzzled. "Who's getting married?"

"We are, I hope," he said.

"Don?" She froze, stunned, not quite sure what was happening.

He laughed. "This is not exactly working out the way I'd planned, but…"

Smiling, he bent down on one knee and took a small box out of his pocket.

"Caitlin Sutherland, I love you, I adore you, and I want to marry you. I want to make babies with you. Not because my mother wants them, but because they'll have your eyes, your smile, your laugh. Hell, I don't mind. They'd be yours. Mine. Ours. Will you be my wife?"

Caitlin's breath had left her body at the word "marry." She inhaled, desperately trying to get some oxygen into her lungs. Her legs refused to keep her upright and she sagged down to her knees in front of him.

"Really?"

Solemnly, he nodded. "Really. I'd foolishly thought that loving you would be enough, but I want to do this, I need to do this. Commitment has always been something I've steered clear of until now. But I want the world to know you'll be my wife."

Caitlin looked down to the ring nestled inside the jeweler's box.

"This is all I could get in Hermanus. But we'll go and find you the biggest diamond there is…"

Caitlin took the ring out and slipped it onto her finger. It fit perfectly. A solitary diamond was flanked by two blue stones. A tear slipped over her cheek.

"Sweetheart, I'll return it immediately, you don't have to keep it…" Don said and tried to take the ring from her finger.

She slapped his hand away and sniffled. "I'm crying because I'm happy, you idiot," she scolded him with a smile. She held out her hand. "This is my ring. You cannot take it back."

"Does that mean you'll marry me?" he asked uncertainly.

Caitlin laughed and threw her arms around his neck. "Of course I'll marry you. I love you. I've loved you from the first time I touched you." She smiled and pulled his head down to hers.

Just before his lips touched hers, she pulled back.

"You know I can't cook?" she asked, biting her lip.

He smiled and kissed her. "It's all right. I can." He rubbed his thumb over her lips. "You know I'm still rich?" he asked.

Caitlin laughed. "I'm getting used to the idea."

***

It was much later when Caitlin's phone rang again. It was her mother. Again. Smiling she answered.

"Yes, Mother, we're getting married!"

Her mother shrieked. "I'm so happy for you, sweetie. When Don asked me, I was a bit worried you'd still have a thing about trusting him, but…"

"Wait a minute? Don asked you? When did he talk to you?" she asked, lifting herself up and looking down at Don. He opened one eye and smiled.

"He was here, early this morning. You were apparently still sleeping," her mother said.

"Anyway, Rosa and I have been talking. We thought it would be a great idea to have the wedding in the Seychelles. We can keep it quiet so that the media can be kept away and—"

"Ooh, Mum, you know, it sounds perfect already and I love it and—" She shot Don a smirk as she pressed the End button on her phone. "She and I can have that very long talk later on, I think."

Don pulled her back on top of him, right where she'd been lying before the phone call.

"Are you happy letting them organize the whole thing?" he asked.

"Very happy." She smiled and moved against him. "It will keep them busy and out of our hair." She bent down to kiss him.

"Good thinking," he said, pulling her so much closer.

EPILOGUE

"I think he's getting too old for this, don't you agree?" David laughed.

"Yeah, I agree. He can't keep up anymore," Dale said.

"Last year he bragged he was going to win the Cape Epic, and look at him now. This is what being married does to you and why you'll never get me near an altar," Darryn muttered.

"Will you shut up and get my wife for me? She should have been here by now," Don growled.

She had been very vague that morning about where she was going and he'd been a bit disappointed. He'd hoped his wife of two months would be at the start of the race. They hadn't been apart since Christmas, he'd made sure of that.

Their mothers had their way and they'd had a wonderful island wedding on Mahé. When Caitlin had walked toward him, he'd fallen in love with her all over again. Dressed in floating, white chiffon, she'd looked exquisite.

"I'm here sweetheart, I'm here." He heard Caitlin's voice behind him and he relaxed.

Then her hands were on his back and he moaned his

pleasure. He couldn't finish the race, something his brothers would probably never ever let him forget, but for once it didn't bother him in the least.

"Caitlin, I think I've also pulled this muscle," Dale whined.

"You know, I'm also a bit sore," David groaned out loud.

"Out, all of you," Don grumbled. "Get your own physios."

Caitlin smiled as her brothers-in-law left the tent. They'd accepted her as part of their family with open arms. Darryn was still a bit wary around her, but she even managed to get a smile out of him now and again.

She was still waiting for Hannah to tell her exactly what had happened between the two of them, and why she still looked scared when she thought no one was watching her, but ever since Christmas there hadn't been time. But Hannah was back from her last photo shoot and Caitlin was meeting her later in the week. Then she was going to insist on hearing the whole story.

But for now, she was focused on her husband's pain.

"I have something to tell you," she said while her fingers worked on his stiff muscles.

He mumbled something incoherent.

"Yes. You may remember that I was skeptical about a cyclist's virility?"

He stilled under her hands.

"Well, I was so wrong. It turns out the saddle has no impact. At all."

Don swung his legs around and sat up straight. He narrowed his eyes.

She swallowed. They hadn't really talked about it, made any plans, since they'd gotten married.

"What are you saying?" He pulled her between his legs.

"Those babies you wanted us to make?" she said,

hesitantly. "Well, it turns out we did."

He inhaled sharply. "And? How do you feel?" he asked, his eyes not giving anything away.

But she knew him. She trusted him.

"I'm so happy."

"Told you I don't have a problem." A huge grin lit up his face. "She's going to have your smile," he said, and tried to lift her up.

"Don, no, your back!" She giggled.

He winced but then she was on his lap. "Not to worry, I have my own personal physio." And then, he was kissing her.

ACKNOWLEDGEMENTS

Thanks to Melissa Keir and Inkspell Publishing for agreeing to publish this story – I so appreciate your help and support during this process.

As always, a big thank you to my husband, Theo who continues to support me and who still reads all my words.

And a big thank you to all the readers who enjoy the stories I write – you are the bonus to an already blessed life.

ABOUT THE AUTHOR

Elsa has been reading love stories for as long as she can remember and when she 'met' the classic authors like Jane Austen, Elizabeth Gaskell, Henry James The Brontë sisters, etc. during her English Honours studies, she was hooked for life.

She married her college boyfriend and soul mate and after 45 years, 3 interesting and wonderful children and 4 beautiful grandchildren, they are now fortunate to live in the picturesque little seaside village of Betty's Bay, South Africa.

She likes the heroines in her stories to be beautiful, feisty, independent and headstrong. And the heroes must be strong but possess a generous amount of sensitivity. They are of course, also gorgeous! Her stories typically incorporate the family background of the characters to better understand where they come from and who they are when we meet them in the story.

Webpage: www.elsawinckler.com
Personal Facebook page:
https://www.facebook.com/elsa.winckler
Author Facebook page:
https://www.facebook.com/ElsaWincklerRomanceAuthor?ref_type=bookmark
Twitter: https://twitter.com/elsawinckler @elsawinckler
Goodreads:
https://www.goodreads.com/author/show/6557709.Elsa_Winckler
Pinterest: http://www.pinterest.com/elsawinckler/
Wattpad: http://www.wattpad.com/user/elsaw1
Instagram: https://www.instagram.com/elsaw1/
Bookbub: https://www.bookbub.com/profile/elsa-winckler